W9-CDH-704

BOOKS BY

NATALIE BABBITT

Dick Foote and the Shark

Phoebe's Revolt

The Search for Delicious

Kneeknock Rise

The Something

Goody Hall

The Devil's Storybook

Tuck Everlasting

The Eyes of the Amaryllis

Herbert Rowbarge

The Devil's Other Storybook

Nellie: A Cat on Her Own

Bub, or The Very Best Thing

Elsie Times Eight

Jack Plank Tells Tales

The Moon Over High Street

THE MOON OVER HIGH STREET

NATALIE BABBITT

THE MOON OVER HIGH STREET

MICHAEL DI CAPUA BOOKS
SCHOLASTIC

Library of Congress control number: 2011926886

Printed in the USA 23

Designed by Kathleen Westray

First edition, 2012

FOR MICHAEL DI CAPUA

ITERUM:

SINE QUO NON

THE
MOON
OVER
HIGH
STREET

I

THIS IS JOE CASIMIR'S story. But if you're going to understand what happened when he got on a bus and came down southwest across the state to visit a town called Midville, you have to know about Mr. Boulderwall.

Mr. Boulderwall was very important in Midville. He'd lived there for a long time—long enough to grow from a watchful little boy, newly arrived from a village in faraway Poland, into a man with a head full of plans. And he made those plans come true. He did it all with his invention of a thing called a "swervit," a thing to be used in engines. It's hard to say where he learned so much about engines, but never mind that. The important thing is that swervits started out unknown, like Mr. Boulderwall himself, and after ten or fifteen years, they were a necessary part of every car, bus, and truck in America. And they made Mr. Boulderwall rich. Very rich. In fact, he was worth millions.

When you're as rich as that, you can afford to live on the best street in town. Every town has a best street. Everything on it is big and beautiful: the houses, the gardens, the trees, even the grass—wide, sweeping lawns of grass, not just patches. Here in America, we like things to be big and beautiful. That's the way the land was in the beginning. That's the way it still is.

Midville's best street was High Street. It was up on a hill. Not much of a hill, to tell the truth, but in that part of the state, the flat south-central part, hills are not taken for granted. Everything on High Street was big, especially the trees. There were a lot of trees, and they were big and very beautiful indeed. But in spite of all that beauty they were like most other trees: In the fall, they dropped their leaves all over everything, making a deep, dry rustle of a mess that had to be raked again and again. *They* didn't care, and why should they? They had their own rules, after all. And anyway, a few of them were so old they'd been on that hill before there even *was* a High Street. Trees don't pay attention to streets. But people do.

Here's the reason why: In America, we like to think we'll own a piece of land someday, maybe even a piece on a street like High Street. If you own a piece of land, you *belong*. Belonging is good, and belonging to what's big and beautiful is about as good as it gets. At least, that's what most of us believe. So we wait and watch and try to find out how to make it happen. Because it *does* happen, all the time, to lots of other people, in lots of other ways besides swervits. So why not make it happen to us? It's all in the knowing how.

There was a lot to learn if you were watching Anson Boulderwall. And by the way, that wasn't the name he was born with. When he was born, in Poland, he was christened Anselm Boldivol. But his mother and father took him away from Poland to escape the endless wars in that part of the world, and they came across the wide Atlantic Ocean, like many thousands of others, to America—where they would be safe. And when he arrived, the first thing he had to do was be taken off the ship at a place called Ellis Island, with everyone else, where he could be weighed and measured. Well, maybe he wasn't exactly weighed and measured, but he was certainly looked at, up, down, and sideways, before they let him come in and be a citizen.

But the people in charge on Ellis Island didn't always pay attention to names. Or maybe they were just so busy looking you over they didn't really listen when you told them who you were. To them, *Anselm* sounded like *Anson*, and *Boldivol* sounded like *Boulderwall*. They wrote it down like that, and that's the way it stayed.

So now, here he was, a long time later, living on High Street with his wife, Ruthetta. She had married him when he was only beginning on the making of swervits; he wasn't rich yet. But Ruthetta—well, let's just say she had a knack for seeing into the future, and for getting what she wanted. When swervits took off in the world of engines and the money was flowing in, she urged and won the move to High Street, and she put all her waiting and watching to the best possible use. She made a few small changes in herself—not unlike the changes a rosebush makes between December and June—and she arranged it so that their only child, a girl they named Ivy, had the necessary extras to guarantee a stylish life: the right schools, the right clothes, piano lessons, and a pony. It worked. Ivy grew up to marry a man who had plenty of money of his own. However, though he didn't object to the fact that Ivy would inherit the Boulderwall fortune someday, he had no interest at all in swervits.

So, what would Mr. Boulderwall do with the factory when he got too old to run it himself? Sell it out of the family? To a *stranger*? Certainly not! It was much too close to his heart. But if not that, then what? The question was always in the back of his mind, and sometimes it even took over the front. That's where it was on the very day when Joe Casimir came to Midville. For it was Mr. Boulderwall's birthday, and he was seventy-one years old and worried about the future. Life always seems to have worries, even if you own a big and beautiful house on the best street in town.

II

Joe Casimir was not in a big and beautiful house on Mr. Boulderwall's birthday. He was on a bus, where he very much didn't want to be. An airplane would have been all right, maybe, but forget about that. Most likely, Midville didn't have an airport, and even if it did, flying cost too much. No, things were the way they had to be, and that was that. Whether he liked it or not, he had to go to Midville to stay with Aunt Myra, he had to go alone, and he had to take the bus.

The trip itself was no surprise. His grandmother—he called her Gran—had planned it for June when school was out. And about time, too, she said. Families should stick together. But she and Joe had only been down to Midville once, and that was years ago. No excuse, she said, when there were just the three of them left. Joe's mother and father had been killed in a car crash when he was no more than a few months old, so he'd always lived with Gran. And his other grandparents—they were gone, too, with him the single grandchild. So this was all that was left of the Casimir family: Gran and Joe and—Aunt Myra.

Aunt Myra wasn't really his aunt. She wasn't anybody's aunt. But she was a cousin of his father's—the same age as his father—so Joe couldn't call her just plain Myra. His grandmother disapproved of young people calling older ones by their first names. However, calling her *Aunt* Myra—that seemed to be all right. Funny how sometimes things were all right even when they were wrong.

Aunt Myra wasn't married, but she had a busy

life in Midville, teaching at some school or other. She'd only come twice to visit them in Willowick—Willowick up north on the edge of Lake Erie, where Joe and his grandmother lived. But Gran said early in the spring, "Joe, if we don't take a trip down to Midville this summer, we'll never get there at all. You're growing up too fast."

Joe had learned long since that if his grandmother wanted things to go a certain way, that's the way they went. Most of the time, this was not a problem. Joe and Gran got along together very well, considering the fact that she was sixty-three years older than he was. They liked to please each other. Still, sometimes he had a certain strong feeling—an irritated feeling—a feeling of having no control over what was going on. He was having that feeling now, on the bus. He found himself wondering why he always had to do what other people wanted. Why should he care about Aunt Myra when he hardly even knew her? But Gran said they had to go to Midville and visit her, so, well, that was that. They had to go to Midville and visit her. June had arrived at last, school was over for the summer, the day for the trip loomed up, and then—this awful thing had happened: Gran was climbing the attic stairs to get a suitcase when she slipped and fell and broke her hip.

Gran wasn't a sissy. She faced up to things the way they were. One of her friends, a widow named Helen Mello, offered to take charge of Joe while the doctors were taking charge of *her*, and for a couple of days she was in no shape for visitors and talking. But after that, when he came to see her: "Joe," she had said in her always sensible voice, "I'm just as sorry as I can be, but you're going to have to go down to Midville by yourself and stay with Aunt Myra while I get over this. I'm going to be perfectly fine, but the doctor says I'll need to be in a recovery sort of place—a rehab center, I think he called it. Anyway, it's special exercises. I'll have to be there for at least a *week*, Joe, until I get going again, and there's nowhere else to *put* you! Unless you want to stay where you are? With Mrs. Mello? No, I didn't think so. But we were going to Midville anyway, after all. I talked to Myra on the phone a couple of hours ago, and she says she really wants to have you there. Then, when I can get around again, I'll go down myself for a few days, and we can come back home together. How does that sound?"

He had told her it sounded all right. It didn't, of course, but if she could face up to things without a fuss, so could he. He spent another night with Mrs. Mello—in a guest room that was mostly ruffles—and in the morning, after breakfast, she made him a peanut-butter sandwich for his lunch and helped him close up his suitcase. And then she took him to the bus station. It was very nice of her, of course, but she made a fuss and she *chirped*, like a sparrow at Gran's old bird feeder. She made a fuss, she chirped, and she kept patting him. And the worst part was, she insisted on pinning a label to the pocket of his shirt, explaining him to the world: *JOSEPH CASIMIR—TO MIDVILLE—WILL BE MET BY MISS MYRA CASIMIR*. "There now!" she chirped, patting him one last time. "You'll have a dandy trip! And when you're on your way, I'll go tell your sweetie of a grandma what a fine, plucky lad you are!" Joe didn't like being called a fine, plucky lad, but he didn't say so. He just swallowed around his irritation, bobbed his head to mean goodbye, and climbed aboard the bus.

Alone at last, he had chosen his seat with care—all the way to the back, and no one to share it. He made sure of that by putting the paper bag with his lunch in it on the seat nearest the aisle. It was a pink paper bag with big white daisies printed on it, exactly the kind of paper bag someone like Mrs. Mello would collect. Under any other circumstances, he'd have hidden it. But now, well, at least people would notice it and not try to sit down next to him. And then, when the bus had left the station, groaning past the eye of Mrs. Mello, he took the label off his pocket, tore it up into very small pieces, and stuffed it into an ashtray in the armrest.

And now he was settling himself for the long angle down southwest across the state with five or six hours ahead of him for thinking. Mostly it was good to have time alone for thinking, but there were questions he couldn't answer, questions that were taking up room in his head and wouldn't go away. What would it be like in Midville? No school, at least, but without it, how could he find someone to talk to? Or was he just supposed to sit in Aunt Myra's living room and stare at the television? And what would Aunt Myra be like? He hadn't seen her for a long, long time. He didn't remember *ever* seeing her. If there were a lot of people waiting to meet the bus, how would he know which one she *was*? How would she know *him*?

He wondered, too, about his friends back in Willowick. What would they be doing while he was gone? Would they wish he was still around? Or would they just yawn and go ahead with summer? Emily Crouse . . . but he decided to try and put her out of his mind. He could get along without Emily Crouse. Of course he could. But he found himself hoping she'd notice he was gone.

And then he told himself it was dumb to think about things like that. After all, he'd be going back pretty soon. But it seemed as if what was happening now must be what it felt like to go away forever.

There was this blank stretch of time, with the old place left behind, when you might as well be no one. You've *been* someone, with people all around who know you, but then you up and leave, and the old place disappears as if it never had been real to begin with. You leave it, and while you're on your way, you feel as if you're disappearing, too. But he didn't have to feel like that. He was only going off for a *little* while. Gran would be okay, and he'd go back to living in Willowick.

He sighed and peered out the window beside him, but there wasn't much to look at. Here, in the country, the land was big, yes, but it certainly wasn't beautiful. Too many tired old farms and scratchy fields cluttering up the view, too many dinky little towns. Behind him, when he looked out the back window, there were only the usual cars and trucks rushing along the highway, once in a while a motorcycle, everyone in a hurry, impatient, wanting to pass the bus.

As well as he could, he craned his neck and squinted upward. Nothing in the sky overhead, as much as he could see of it. Just ordinary clouds and sunshine. He sighed again and wished with all his heart that it was nighttime. There were always good things to look at then, up there, things that magically eased him of the irritated feeling. And someday, when he was on his own—well, but never mind that now. Someday was a long way off. Tonight was not a long way off. And Midville would have a night sky; that much was certain. But first he had to get there.

He settled deeper into his seat, and now and then he almost went to sleep. Outside the window, more of the same farms and fields and little towns. Once in a while a city with stops to let passengers off, passengers on. He didn't want to look at the passengers. He'd brought along a couple of books, and pretended to be busy reading, but really reading on a bus, a bus that swayed—no, not a good idea. He ate the peanut-butter sandwich and finished off the bottle of ginger ale. He tried to play that alphabet game where you had to find all the letters, *capital* letters, in order from *A* to *Z*, on the billboards and signs beside the highway, but finally it only made him even more irritated. Most of the letters on the way to *Q* were easy to spot, but you'd think there was some kind of law against using a *Q* word on a billboard. After half an hour, he gave it up.

More long gray miles of fields and shabby farms, another tiresome stretch of trying not to think. And then, all at once, the driver called out: "Next stop, Midville! *Midville next!*" Joe sat up, suddenly a little breathless, suddenly alert. He lifted his suitcase onto his lap, keeping a grip on the handle. "Maybe it won't be so bad," he told himself. "Not *too* bad, anyway." He sat erect and looked out the window, really looked this time, to see what it was like. Simple little houses, strewn wide apart, then a railroad track, a bridge across a narrow river. Warehouses, storage tanks, factories tucked behind chain-link fences. More railroad tracks. Then a much bigger factory, with tidy trucks lined up, and a big, tidy sign on its roof: SWERVIT, INC. Now all of this giving way to fancier buildings—offices, department stores, restaurants. Friday afternoon sidewalks full of shoppers. The bus growled into a station and lurched to a stop. The driver stood up, rubbing his shoulders. And then he turned and called, "Okay, kid, this is you."

The aisle was suddenly full of passengers gathering packages and magazines and every kind of luggage, making a bustle. Joe struggled out of the safety of his seat, his own suitcase hanging heavy from his grip. He waited till the aisle was clear and then, slowly, abandoning the pink paper bag, he went to the open door. His heart was pounding and his face was hot, for all at once he felt like something ordered through the mail that might turn out to be wrong. He climbed down the tall pair of steps and stood on concrete, bewildered. Late afternoon sunshine burned on his head, the push of people made him blink. He set his suitcase at his feet and rubbed his nose. "What if no one comes?" he wondered vaguely.

And then, hurrying toward him, he saw a tall woman with a broad, beaming face. "Joe!" she cried, waving an arm. "Here I am, Joe!" And he found himself wrapped close in an ample, warm embrace. "Joe," said the voice in his ear, softly now, "I'm Myra. Welcome, Joe. I'm so glad you're here!"

III

"HERE WE GO," said Aunt Myra. "This way. My car's right over there. So—how was your trip?"

"It was okay," said Joe, trying not to lose her on the crowded sidewalk.

"A long time to sit on a bus, though," she said. "Well, never mind. It's over now. You don't remember much about *this* place, do you? You were only two or three last time you came."

"I guess," said Joe. And then he waited, expecting her to tell him what a cute little boy he'd been.

But, wonder of wonders, she didn't. "You'll learn your way around in no time" was all she said. "It's simple." And then: "Here we are." She dumped his suitcase into the trunk of her little black Ford, and then they were off, down streets, around corners, all a blur for Joe. Downtown gave way to streets for people. Yards with trees. A square brick building with a flagpole in front: "That's the school where I teach," she told him. "Lincoln School." Around another corner, past more houses. A little grocery store. And then, suddenly, a park! Bigger trees. A slide—and swings and seesaws. A baseball diamond. And a bandstand! An honest-to-goodness bandstand! Not too bad, all that. Around a final corner, up a second block, and "Here we are! Number 24 Glen Lane." They bounced into the driveway and Joe found himself in front of a small clapboard house that was not so different from his grandmother's—a friendly little two-story house with a porch across the front and what might be a pretty good yard out back. It looked as if—well, as if it wouldn't want much from him. As if it would take him as he was. And he let out a long breath.

And then: He had climbed out of the Ford and was standing looking up and down the quiet street when all at once the quiet was erased. Here came a rattling white van, its purpose emblazoned on its side in large green letters: SOPE ELECTRIC. Under this was painted a jagged bolt of lightning and the words *RESIDENTIAL AND COMMERCIAL*, the whole finished off with *NO JOB TOO SMALL*. "Hey!" said Aunt Myra. "Here come my neighbors!"

The van bumped into the driveway of a shingled house across the street, a door rumbled open, and four people of various sizes rolled out like an upset pile of melons. Aunt Myra named them as they appeared: Evangeline Sope, aged six, in full shriek. Dorothea Sope, aged nine, blowing a cardboard horn of the birthday-party variety, which made a lovely blatting sound. Beatrice Sope, aged twelve, managing three huge blue balloons. Finally, Ogilvie Sope, father of all and calm as a millpond, stepping over and around them only to be nearly toppled by a joyful rush of fur that was large and devoted Rover Sope, dog of all, just released from inside the house by Amanda Sope, mother and wife. At the house door, mother and father embracing and mother crying to the tumbled group, "How was the party?" Three answers, all different except for volume, all coming at once.

"Let's go over," said Aunt Myra. "I'll introduce you."

It would be a while before Joe remembered their names, but for now none of them was really important. None, that is, except Beatrice.

"This is Beatrice, Joe," said Aunt Myra. "She's just your age."

"Hi," said Beatrice.

As for Joe, all he could do was mumble. For Beatrice Sope was beautiful, with a round, clear face, and hair as dark and shiny as fine furniture. Joe looked away and swallowed hard. In the back of his mind, where he had stowed them on the bus, thoughts of Emily Crouse wavered, dimmed, and disappeared. His face went flaming red. He found that he needed to cough, and began to believe that he'd always known Midville would be fine.

•

In Aunt Myra's house, there was a front hall and then a living room with a long, loose-cushioned sofa, a coffee table and a couple of armchairs, a lot of plants in pots, and shelves full of books. There was a kitchen with the usual stove and refrigerator, a table for eating, and more plants in pots on a windowsill. And then off the kitchen was another room. "There's a guest room upstairs, next to my room," Aunt Myra told Joe, "and I thought I'd put Gran there and let you have this, so you and she don't have to share. But when she gets here she may have trouble going up and down the stairs, what with that busted hip. So we'll have to see. This might be better for her then. But for now it's yours."

It was small, but it held a lot: a low bed with two fat pillows, an armchair covered in blue corduroy, a maple bureau with plenty of drawers, and, next to that, a desk with its own chair. Light blue curtains framed the windows that, side by side, looked out to the backyard. There was even a little bookcase, its wide shelves empty and waiting. Joe stood in the doorway, speechless. It was the best room he had ever seen, and it was his.

Behind him, Aunt Myra said, "Does it look all right? It used to be my sewing room, but, shoot, I don't have time for sewing. I'm over at school all day long."

Joe set down his suitcase and searched for words. And then, at last, he managed to say, "It's just—well, it's really—good."

Aunt Myra smiled. It seemed to be enough.

•

THAT NIGHT, after a supper of pizza and ice cream ("But I don't want you to think we'll eat like this every night," said Aunt Myra), Joe unpacked his suitcase and put his clothes away while she sat in the corduroy chair, telling stories about Midville with pauses in between, funny little pauses where she looked out the windows, wanting, he suddenly suspected, to talk about something very different but seeming uncertain how to begin.

With all his clothes in their places, Joe, with nothing more to do, sat down on the bed to wait. He was sure it would come now, whatever it was she wanted to say, and while he was waiting, he looked at her, really looked at her, for the first time. She was tall—well, he'd noticed that at first—and her hair was ordinary brown cut short and wavy around a plain, uncomplicated face, a regular in-between face except for her eyes, which were full of feeling.

"Joe," she said at last, "you don't remember your father, do you?"

"No," he said. This was it, then, what she wanted to say. He looked away, down at the floor, and the irritated feeling filled him completely.

But she went on: "I remember him. We had the same grandparents, and we were just about the same age. We used to see each other on holidays." There was another pause, and then she said, speaking quickly, "He was a good person, Joe. I liked him a lot. I went to his wedding, when he married your mother. Listen, Joe, I'm not going to go on and on about this. I just need to tell you that after that terrible accident, I wanted you, Joe. I was alone, too, all of a sudden, just like you. Gran had a perfect right to keep you—your father's mother, after all—and I was only a second cousin or something. But, Joe, I wanted you. I've always wanted you. That's why it makes me so happy to have you here now."

"Okay," said Joe, keeping his eyes on the floor.

"All right," said Aunt Myra. She leaned toward him, and for a moment he was afraid she was going to kiss him, but she only gave him a quick touch on the shoulder. She stood up and said, "Well, good night. Sleep well."

Then, as she was going to the door, the irritated feeling erupted and he heard himself say, suddenly, "How come you never got married, Aunt Myra? Didn't anyone ask you?" And at once he wished with all his heart he hadn't said it. It sounded bad. Bad—and mean.

But she didn't seem to mind. She paused in the doorway and turned. "I was going to get married," she told him. "We were engaged. But he was killed in the war. Korea."

Joe heard these words with amazement. Somehow he'd never thought about other people having losses, too. His irritation disappeared. He said, "I'm sorry, Aunt Myra! I really am sorry! What was his name?"

Her face softened. "His name," she said with a little smile, "was Joe."

"Oh!" he said. "Like me."

"Yes," she answered. "Like you. Good night."

•

AND THEN HE WAS alone. He went to a window and peered out. The last of the twilight still rimmed the sky, late though it was, for these were the longest days. And the air was still balmy. Even so, Joe shivered a little. It had been a whole lot more of a day than he was used to. But there was a night sky here, all right, just as he'd known there would be. There weren't a lot of stars to look at yet, but they were up there. They'd come out soon. So would the moon.

And crickets had begun their songs. Out in his yard, Rover Sope was barking his friendly good-nights to all the dogs in Midville. And Aunt Myra—Aunt Myra had said, "I've always wanted you." The warmth of these things was very fine, and almost the finest of all was that picture in another part of his head: the late-day sun on the shiny hair of the girl across the street.

IV

Saturday morning. Joe woke suddenly, his eyes wide. And then: Oh! This was *Midville*, so it was all right. When he was up and ready, he went to the kitchen. On the stove a frying pan was sending out promising sizzles and pops while Aunt Myra stirred something smooth and creamy in a big bowl. "Pancakes and bacon, Joe," she said. "Hope you like them." Like them! Who didn't? "Of course, it's not a skinny breakfast," she added, "but we'll get around to that later."

There was orange juice, too, and butter and maple syrup, and they sat down to it and began to eat as if they'd been together every morning of their lives, handing the butter and the syrup back and forth like friends for whom no words are necessary. Still, it was the *first* breakfast and both of them knew this very well, though neither of them said so. At one point, Joe sensed her looking at him, and he lifted his eyes to her face. She turned away quickly, but she was smiling.

And then, just as they were finishing, the telephone rang. It was a wall phone, hanging near the stove, and Aunt Myra got up to answer it. "Hello? . . . Oh, hi, Gil . . . It's Mr. Sope," she told Joe over her shoulder. "What? . . . Oh, that sounds wonderful! I think he'd . . . Yes, but he doesn't have a bicycle here, so maybe . . . Gil, you don't have to do that . . . Well, wait a minute while I ask him." She put the phone down and turned to Joe. "Beatrice wants to take you around town and show you things. Would you like that? Mr. Sope says you can borrow his bicycle. And the two of you can get your lunch somewhere if you're gone that long. What do you think?"

"All right," said Joe. Beatrice? All morning on bicycles? Yes. He thought it would be all right. And Aunt Myra hadn't told him he had to go; she had asked him if he wanted to. She had let it be his decision.

•

"THIS IS A PRETTY good town," said Beatrice as they pedaled down the street, Rover loping along beside them. "But I've never lived anywhere else, so I haven't got much to compare it to. What's your hometown like?"

"It's okay," said Joe. "Not so different from here, I guess." Except he didn't think he'd ever seen a Willowick sky as blue as this. Or a Willowick sun this bright. It winked through the trees to splash on the blacktop and the handlebars of Beatrice's bicycle. And on her shiny hair. But of course he didn't say all that out loud.

"You've got Lake Erie, though," she said. "We

don't have anything like that. I've hardly ever even seen Lake Erie. You're lucky. And you get to go around alone. I almost never get to do that. I mean, *someone* has to look after Evangeline and Dorothea once in a while. Mother can't do everything. You don't have any brothers or sisters, do you?"

"No," he said.

"You're lucky," she repeated. "See, the thing is—wait a minute—where's Rover?" She braked to a stop, looking around, and Joe stopped beside her. "There he is. Rats! I wish he wouldn't always do this. Just look at him! He's been rolling in Junior Johnson's wading pool again."

Rover had come briskly into the front yard of a nearby house. He was soaked and dripping, the long hairs on his chest and tail plastered to his skin, his ears like wet washcloths. He looked, this way, to be a thin dog of no importance. But, pausing near a bed of hyacinths, he took a firm stance and shook himself, transferring a fine rain out of his coat and onto the flowers, and was once again a dog of substance. "Rover," said Beatrice as he came smiling up to them, "you're very bad." But she didn't sound really angry. Rover seemed to recognize this because he went right on smiling in that way some big dogs have where the ears will droop, the eyes go soft, and the generous lips turn up at their generous corners.

"What kind of a dog is he?" asked Joe, looking at him with approval.

"Well, let's see," said Beatrice. "He's half golden retriever, half Airedale, and half cocker spaniel."

"That's three halves!" Joe pointed out.

"Yep," she said. "That's why he's so big. But he's really only a mutt. Like all of us Sopes."

"You think you're mutts?" said Joe in astonishment.

"Sure," said Beatrice, laughing. "It only means you haven't got a pedigree. But Pop says what good is a pedigree unless you like standing around being looked at."

They started off again, in and out of neighboring streets, and crisscrossed the park Joe had noticed the day before. Beatrice even took him to the junior high school. "You'll have to go to one, too, won't you?"

she asked him as they paused at the curb in front. "It'll be awful. We'll be the youngest ones, just like first grade. Probably get pushed around a lot."

"I guess so," said Joe.

"Of course," she added as they started off again, "I've always been the oldest at my house. That makes it harder. But Miss Myra told us about you once, so I know you're the oldest *and* the youngest at your house. It's like I started to say before. You're lucky. You've got a lot of independence."

Lucky! She'd said three times that he was lucky. It was a description so different from the way he saw himself that he hardly knew how to answer. But she wasn't waiting for an answer. "Hey!" she said. "Want to go up on the hill and see where the rich people live? No mutts on High Street! The houses are practically castles. There's a boy in my class that lives up there, but he's going to Glenfield next year."

"What's Glenfield?" Joe asked her.

"It's a private school for boys," she explained. "There's one for girls, too, called Folkestone. They're both out in the country."

"Oh," said Joe.

"It's not a big deal," she told him. "It's just what you have to do if you're rich. Come on. If you want to know about Midville, you need to see High Street. And then we can go get lunch."

•

YES, THE HOUSES WERE big and beautiful, with big and beautiful trees and wide green lawns. Some had low stone walls along the front and—but wait: "Wow!" said Joe. "Look at *that* one!"

They climbed off their bikes and stood on the sidewalk, gazing at it. It was set far back from the street, on an even wider, greener lawn. A big, very beautiful house: white-painted brick with black trim and shutters, and a row of white pillars across the front.

Beatrice said, "That's where Mr. Boulderwall lives. He owns that factory over on the other side of town."

"He must be really rich," said Joe.

"Yep," she answered. "He invented those engine things called swervits. His factory's the only place in the world that makes them, but Pop told me they're used all over everywhere."

"I've heard of those," said Joe. "My grandmother had to get a new one for her car last winter." And then, still gazing, he said, almost to himself, "I wonder what it's like to live in a house like that."

Beatrice nodded. "But think if you had to clean it every week!" she said. "Of course, they must have lots of maids to do that kind of stuff. It's hard to picture Mrs. Boulderwall running a vacuum cleaner."

"Do you know her?" he asked.

"I don't exactly *know* her," she said, "but I've seen her lots of times. Pop did some work for them once, putting in a bunch of outside lights. He said there's a swimming pool way out back, and a tennis court, and . . . oh *no*! Rover! *ROVER!*"

Too late. It was as if Rover Sope had heard the word *pool* and knew what it suggested. He galloped away across the lawn, ignoring Beatrice's calls and whistles, and disappeared behind the house. "This is the absolute worst!" said Beatrice. "Now what are we going to do? We'll have to go get him—we can't just leave him. But what if someone's back there? What if they see us?"

"Or what if he gets in the swimming pool?" said Joe.

"Oh—that's a terrible idea!" said Beatrice. "You're right, of course. It's just what he *will* do, the dummy, and then he might not be able to get out again. I mean, it's a real *swimming* pool, with a deep end and everything. Come on—hurry!"

They dropped their bikes and ran.

•

HAPPILY, THE WORST isn't always what happens. Behind the house, there was a wide flagstone terrace with red-cushioned wicker chairs and lounges set about and a round white metal table shaded by a tilting striped umbrella. Sitting at the table was Anson Boulderwall himself, the Saturday morning newspapers spread out around him. At his elbow was a tray with coffee and a plate of cinnamon sweet rolls, and he was sharing a roll with Rover.

He was certainly old. Joe's first impression was

that he looked like one of those drawings a little child might make: a round body, with long, thin arms and legs stuck on like sticks poked into an apple. Under the summer fabric of his white shirt and trousers, his elbows, knees, and shoulders made sharp angles. The backs of his wrinkled hands were dotted with large brown spots, and the knuckles made more angles as he gripped the sweet roll and tore off chunks of it for Rover. But there was something far more important about him than the fact that he was old—something calm and solid and powerful.

Rover knew power when he met with it. Dogs always do. He was sitting pressed close to the old man's knee, ears high, muzzle dusted with sugar, his eyes full of respect—and hope. "Well!" said Mr. Boulderwall as Beatrice and Joe came up to him. "This your animal?"

"Oh dear," said Beatrice. "Yes, he's mine. I'm really sorry he bothered you. I tried to call him back, but he wouldn't come."

"He's not a bother," said Mr. Boulderwall. "I like dogs. You two live around here?"

"Over on Glen Lane," said Beatrice. "I was showing Joe the town. He's new here."

Mr. Boulderwall looked at Joe. "Oh? Your family just move in?" he asked.

"No," said Joe. "I'm visiting my . . . uh . . . aunt."

"Where's your family, then?" asked Mr. Boulderwall.

"I don't . . . I mean, there isn't . . . except for my grandmother and my aunt, I'm all there is," said Joe, but he said it with a frown. It was none of this old man's business.

If Mr. Boulderwall noticed Joe's discomfort, he brushed it aside. "So, what you're saying is, you're more or less an orphan. Right? Except for your aunt?"

"She's not exactly my aunt," Joe mumbled. "She's just a cousin or something."

"She's a really nice person," Beatrice put in. "She's a teacher now, but she used to work for my father at Sope Electric."

"Aha! Your father runs Sope Electric?" said Mr. Boulderwall, glancing at Beatrice.

"Yes," she said, and then: "Oh, excuse me, Mr. Boulderwall! We know who *you* are, of course, but you don't know us. I'm Beatrice Sope. And this is Joe Casimir."

The old man paused. His eyes widened and he turned in his chair to get a better look at Joe. And then after a moment he said, "Your name is Casimir? How do you spell that?"

Joe swallowed, and coughed, and looked up into a nearby elm tree. "C-A-S-I-M-I-R," he said, and coughed again.

Mr. Boulderwall took a sip of coffee without taking his eyes away from Joe's face. "It's a Polish name," he said at last, putting down his cup. "Did you know that?"

"I guess not," said Joe.

"Well, it is," he said. "There were some kings in Poland with that name, a long time back. So your father's people must have been Polish. What's your aunt's name? Or your cousin, or whatever. The woman you're staying with?"

"She's Myra Casimir."

He squinted at Joe for a moment, and then: "How old are you, boy?" he asked.

Beatrice glanced at Joe and then gave the answer for him. "He's twelve, just like me," she said.

Mr. Boulderwall kept his eyes on Joe. "Twelve," he repeated. He scratched idly behind one of Rover's ears. "Your dog's wet," he said to Beatrice, without looking at her.

"I know," she said. "He got into someone's wading pool. We'd better take him home now, Mr. Boulderwall. Thank you for being so patient with him. I'll make sure he doesn't come in here again."

"He's welcome any time," said the old man. "All three of you are welcome." And then he turned back abruptly to his newspaper.

•

OUT ON THE SIDEWALK, Beatrice said, "Phew! I'm glad that's over!"

"Me, too," said Joe with feeling.

"Well, let's take Rover back and go get lunch at the Gobble House."

"Gobble House?" said Joe. "There's a Gobble House here? We've got one of those at home."

"They're all over the place," said Beatrice. Then, as they pedaled off, she added, "Mr. Boulderwall was nice about Rover, though. And the way he kept looking at you, I think he really liked you."

While she was saying this, Anson Boulderwall, alone at the round metal table, pushed the Saturday papers aside and took from a pocket a small, leather-covered notebook. He slid its tiny pencil out of the loop attached, opened the notebook, and printed *JOE CASIMIR*. Then, underneath that, he added *MYRA CASIMIR*. When this was done, he tore the slip of paper out of the notebook and laid it on the table in front of him. And then, for a long time, he sat there thinking.

•

AT LUNCH IN THE BIG and beautiful house, Mrs. Boulderwall helped herself to a salad of cold shrimp from a platter being offered by a maid in a cap and apron. "Thank you, Delia," she said to the maid, and waved her on to Mr. Boulderwall. And then: "Anson," she asked, "didn't I see a boy and girl out on the terrace with you? That dreadful animal was theirs, I suppose. What in the world did they want?"

"They didn't want anything," he told her. "They were just trying to get the dog back." And then he said, "The boy's name is Casimir."

"What kind of a name is that?" she said. "I don't know anyone with a name like that!"

"I didn't either, not until now," he said, looking off with a thoughtful frown. "Not still alive, anyway. There were three kings of Poland called Casimir. I *think* it was three. Way, way back. *Hundreds* of years ago. This boy is visiting an aunt here—or some relative or other. Her name is . . . uh . . . just a minute." He took the slip of paper out from an inside pocket and glanced at it. "Oh yes. *Myra* Casimir. She lives on Glen Lane. And his name is Joe." He paused, and then became his regular, brisk, decided self again. "Ruthetta, I want you to do me a favor. Invite them to come over here tomorrow, just the two of them. For tea or something. You'll have to send a note right away. Fergus can take it and wait for an answer." He handed the slip of paper across to her and added, thoughtfully, "I need to get to know that boy."

Mrs. Boulderwall narrowed her eyes. "Anson, what's this all about?"

"Maybe nothing. I don't know yet," he told her. "It's just an idea."

She frowned. "But what in the world could you possibly want with an ordinary boy like that? I mean, where does he come from? Who are his people? Are you telling me you want to invite him here, to the house? As a guest?"

"That's what I'm telling you," said Mr. Boulderwall.

"But, Anson, surely you don't think, just because he's got the same name as some dead Polish king . . ."

"If you mean do I think he's got royal blood in him, of course I don't!" said Mr. Boulderwall. "Didn't I ever tell you about the welder, down at the factory, named Abe Lincoln? No relation at all. No, I just want to see that boy again, is all. So set it up, please, Ruthetta. Tomorrow. For tea. I'll find the right address and tell Fergus to get out the car. And when you've got the note ready, give it to him and he'll do the rest." They finished their lunch in silence and then he stood up, stretched, came around the table to kiss her cheek, and left the dining room.

Mrs. Boulderwall rearranged a kiss-disturbed curl at the side of her carefully cut gray hair. All right: If getting to know that boy up close was what her husband wanted, she supposed she could manage it for him. It was certainly a little peculiar, but probably harmless. Still, she shook her head. In spite of her husband's obvious success in matters of business, he did seem to have these *notions* sometimes. And there was never much use in her trying to guide him back to common sense. Oh, well. Tea, then. She went to her desk in the library and, while Delia cleared away the luncheon things, sat down to a sheet of her best stationery and wrote the necessary note.

V

Joe came back to Glen Lane with a good opinion of life. Hamburgers with Beatrice at the Gobble House had been perfect. So was the trip home. And Beatrice told him he could borrow her father's bicycle whenever he wanted—that maybe next time they could go out into the country and look around. So who cared if his Willowick friends didn't miss him? He didn't miss them. Not now. He found himself humming under his breath and walked into Aunt Myra's house as if he'd always lived there.

Aunt Myra was in the living room with a tall, bony man who was perched on the arm of a chair at one end of the sofa, a man with a thin, cheerful, wide-awake face who seemed watchful and ready, as if he was expecting something. "Joe!" said Aunt Myra. "Good—you're back! Here's someone I want you to meet. Vinnie, this is my cousin, Joe. Joe, this is Vinnie Fortunado. He's the Number Two man down at Sope Electric."

"Hey, kid," said Vinnie. "Yeah, I was in the neighborhood, and I just come by for a minute. So—ya took the boss's daughter out, that so? Where'd ya go?"

There was something about Vinnie that Joe liked right away, something that made it easy to talk. "We rode bicycles all over," he said, sitting down beside Aunt Myra, "and then she took me up to that street with all those really big houses. And while we were up there, her dog, Rover, ran into the backyard of some people named Boulderwall. We had to go behind the house to get him. Rover, I mean. And *he* was out there. Mr. Boulderwall."

"Well, well," said Vinnie. "Big Bucks Boulderwall."

Aunt Myra's eyes were round. "You really met him, Joe? What was he like?"

"He was all right," said Joe. "He was giving a cinnamon roll to Rover. But he asked me a lot of questions. I mean, he wanted to know how I spell my name, and—"

Then an interruption: somebody knocking at the door.

"Must be the mailman," said Aunt Myra. "Will you get it, please, Joe? And hurry back! I want to hear more about your morning."

But it wasn't the mailman who had knocked—at least, not any kind of mailman Joe had ever seen. When he went down the hall and opened the door, he found a hunched little man in a trim dark suit and cap standing on the porch—a very polite little man who touched the bill of his cap in a kind of salute and said, "Good afternoon. My name is Fergus. I'm sorry to trouble you, but I have a letter here from Mrs. Anson Boulderwall for Miss Myra Casimir." At the curb a long, dark blue car was waiting—a very shiny car looking as out of place on Glen Lane as a yacht in a duck pond.

"Aunt Myra," Joe called over his shoulder, "it's for you."

She came, curious, and stood at the open door.

"Good afternoon, ma'am," said the little man, with a second salute. "I hope you're well today. My name is Fergus, and I'm the driver for Mr. and Mrs. Anson Boulderwall. I have a message for you, and I'm hoping I'll be able to take a reply back with me. If that would be convenient?"

This was clearly a question. "Well," said Aunt Myra, "of course! Certainly! Won't you come in?"

Fergus stepped back a little and shook his head. "Oh—no, thank you, ma'am. I'll wait right here. And," he added kindly, holding out an envelope, "there's no need to hurry. Please take your time."

The envelope was made of heavy, cream-colored paper. She opened it carefully and, sitting down on the sofa with Joe on one side and Vinnie on the other, she unfolded a single heavy, cream-colored sheet at the top of which were the initials *RB* engraved in blue. And then, below that, the handwritten message. She read it aloud:

Dear Miss Casimir,

It would give my husband and me the greatest pleasure if you and Joseph would join us for tea tomorrow, Sunday, at four o'clock in the afternoon. We'll be outside if the weather stays so lovely. We've been lucky, haven't we, with the springtime this year!

We are looking forward so much to meeting you.

Sincerely,
Ruthetta Boulderwall

Aunt Myra dropped the letter into her lap. "Joe! What on earth!" she exclaimed. "You must have made a really good impression on Mr. Boulderwall this morning!" She picked up the letter and read it again, to herself this time, and her face showed a mix of doubt and dismay. "I have to answer this right away," she said, "so that poor man out there won't have to stand around. What do you think, Joe? Seems to me we pretty much have to say yes. I mean, it's the *Boulderwalls*! Would you mind?"

Joe frowned. "But I didn't do anything up there! I hardly said a word! Do we really have to go?"

And Vinnie snorted. "If ya don't wanna go, ya just say, no, thanks! Simple as that. Ya don't hafta do what they tell ya. It's not like they was royalty or somethin'."

"Now, Vinnie," said Myra, "I'm sure they don't think they're royalty! This is just an invitation to tea. You've never met them, you don't have any idea what they're really like."

"I've sort of met 'em," he declared. "I done alotta work up there on High Street. And anyway, you don't know 'em, either!"

"No," she said, "but it seems to me they're being perfectly nice. What have you got against rich people? I thought *you* wanted to be rich! You keep talking about winning the lottery."

"That's right," said Vinnie. "It'll happen, too. Wait and see."

"Would you get a whole lot of money if you

won?" asked Joe, forgetting for the moment the question of tea with the Boulderwalls.

"Listen, kid," said Vinnie, leaning forward and stabbing the coffee table with a skinny finger, "it's not *if* I win, it's *when*. And yeah, you bet it'll be a whole lotta money! I haven't made up my mind yet what I'm gonna do with it. Not exactly, anyway. But I know this much. When it happens, I'm gonna go through the rest of my life with a great big smile on my face." And he sat back with a firm nod of satisfaction.

"How come you're so sure you'll win?" Joe asked him.

"When ya know somethin', kid," said Vinnie with finality, "ya *know* it. But listen. When it happens, it ain't gonna turn me inta someone else. I'll still be just plain Vinnie Fortunado, same as now. See, that's the thing about High Street people. They act like they're the only ones with a ticket t'the show. But march 'em around in their underwear, ya can see they ain't no different from anybody else. People is people."

"My grandmother says the same thing," Joe

told him. "I mean, that everyone's the same underneath."

Vinnie stood up. "Well, kid," he said, "I ain't no grandmother, but, in my experience, that's about the size of it. So, see ya around, Myra. Have a good vacation." And he went down the hall and out the door, closing it with a bang behind him.

"What did he mean about a vacation?" Joe asked her.

"Oh, just that school is closed for the summer," she explained. "And I have some ideas of things we could do, you and I. But, Joe, before we talk about that, we have to decide about tomorrow." She picked up Mrs. Boulderwall's note from the coffee table and put it back into its envelope. "Don't you think we'd better say yes to this invitation? I know you don't want to, but—well, it would be fun to see that house."

"I saw it," he said. "It's just a house."

"It seems like a whole lot more than just a house!" she said. "And to tell you the truth, the idea of going up there scares me half to death. But if we went together—oh, Joe, let's do it! It's just this one time. People like us almost never get invited anywhere by people like the Boulderwalls. We won't stay long." She looked at him pleadingly, adding, "We'd have to go out and buy you a shirt and necktie, but you wouldn't mind getting dressed up, would you? It's sort of like a uniform for parties—you know? So, how about it? Shall I tell them we're coming?"

"Oh . . . well," said Joe, "okay. If you really want to." He was able to say this, to put his own wishes aside and agree, because all at once he felt as if he were the grown-up, weary with experience of the world, and she were the eager child who needed him to show it to her.

•

THEY WENT downtown after supper, to the boys' section of a large department store—Dapper's by name—and came away into the twilight with a manly white shirt and a necktie that was dark blue with little yellow stars all over it. Aunt Myra had chosen it from all the dozens hanging on the rack, and as they headed for home and were pausing at a stop sign, she pointed up at the sky. "Look, Joe—it's just like your necktie!"

And so it was: dark blue, and now, out here beyond the downtown competition, the little yellow stars were showing themselves, sprinkled wide across that blue like grains of salt. "Joe," said Aunt Myra, pulling away from the stop sign, "would it be all right if we drove just a little ways out in the country? Before we go home? Maybe it sounds silly, but sometimes I like to look at the night sky."

"Sure," he said, trying not to show his surprise. "Go ahead." And then he was about to add, "I like it, too," but he stopped himself just in time. It was something he never talked about. He didn't know why, exactly, except that it seemed too *private*, like something only he would understand, so that a door closed in his head when anyone came too near, a door with a sign that said to him: KEEP YOUR MOUTH SHUT.

Beyond the city limits they went, and out to where streetlights were few and far between, where in the dimness the little farms had settled quietly behind rail fences, where cowsheds and hay barns were turning into comfortable shapes resting in their own shadows. The animals had settled, too: not a cackle or a moo to be heard when Aunt Myra pulled her car to the roadside near one of the farms and turned off the engine. The moon had appeared from behind a cloud while they were on their way, and now its gentle face hung glowing nearly full, low in the sky. "It's so fine!" said Aunt Myra. And then, after a pause: "There was a time once when I wanted to be—oh, an astronomer, I guess—*you* know, study the stars, if you can imagine a thing like that."

He could. He could imagine it easily. But all he said was "I guess so."

She sighed. "It would've taken a lot of time," she said. "Learning all that science, I mean. And maybe it would've been too hard, anyway. I never much caught on to algebra in school. Things with formulas, things you have to prove with fractions and those funny little symbols. *You* know. You do a proof, but when you're finished, you don't know *what* you've proved, and you don't know *why*. Oh, well, a person doesn't have to get an A in math to come out and look at the stars!"

"No," said Joe. Still, he kind of liked things with formulas—fancy arithmetic, what little he'd had of it in classes so far—but maybe this wasn't the time to say so. Not yet. Instead, he said, "You could go back to school. If you wanted to."

"What a notion!" she said with a laugh. "No, I'm very happy doing what I'm doing, thank you." They sat for a while after that, both of them quiet, gazing upward. Then, at last, she switched on the engine of the car. "Time to head home," she said. "The sky will have to do without us for the rest of tonight."

But the stars—and the moon—would still be there, Joe said to himself with satisfaction. They were always there whether anyone looked at them or not.

VI

THE NEXT AFTERNOON, Joe looked at himself in the mirror. He'd hardly ever had a necktie on before. But at least this one was pre-tied—he hadn't had to ask for help to make it look the way it was supposed to. And it wasn't all that bad, he decided, turning this way and that. It just looked like a costume for a play, was all. That's what it felt like, anyway, going to the Boulderwalls' for tea: being in a play. He wondered what Gran would say if she could see him. And then he wondered what Beatrice would say. Well, never mind. He was glad neither one of them had to see him today because he'd probably do everything wrong. Spill his tea or something. But at least the costume looked all right.

He could hear Aunt Myra upstairs in her room, moving around, opening and shutting her bureau drawers and her closet again and again. He came into the living room and plunked himself down on the sofa to wait for her. And then—a distant grumbling from the edges of a sky gone moody, and the first tap-tap of raindrops. There'd be no sitting safely outside at the Boulderwalls'. They'd have to go inside the big and beautiful house.

•

AT EXACTLY four o'clock, with Aunt Myra carefully dressed in a dark brown skirt and jacket, they stood at the Boulderwalls' big front door and she rang the bell. At once the door swung open and a maid in a crisp uniform was beckoning them to come inside to a wide central hall. It was a softly lit hall, with a tall vase of taller white roses standing on a narrow table.

On the wall behind the table, an immense and heavy mirror framed in fussy gilt curlicues frowned out at them as if to say they should keep their reflections to themselves. At the farther end of the hall, a deeply carpeted staircase curved upward to more soft light. And down here where they stood, wide arches led to—what? Never mind. They were directed to the room on the left. A living room. Except, Joe thought to himself, you couldn't really *live* in a room like this.

"Please sit down," said the maid. "I'll tell Mrs. Boulderwall you're here."

She came, in flowered silk with a cashmere cardigan sweater tossed across her shoulders. She came with a smile, her head tilted back and her eyes half shut, and she took Aunt Myra's hand in the warmest of gestures. "My dear Miss Casimir!" she said. "How good of you! And you, too, Joseph." Behind her, Mr. Boulderwall appeared, his eyes going at once to Joe, though he, too, shook Aunt Myra's hand. Another maid was there now with a heavy silver tray displaying a gleaming silver tea service. Two teapots, one big, one small. A lidded sugar bowl with tongs.

A cream pitcher. Silver spoons. Teacups and saucers of the thinnest, most delicate china. Little napkins embroidered with a single initial: *B*. And a platter of sweets: butter wafers, macaroons, and thin-sliced brownies.

It was exactly what Joe had expected. The indoors was just as perfect as the outdoors, except that here, indoors, it all looked careful, somehow. Too careful. Everything matched. Everything fit. Everything had been chosen to bring out the best in everything else. The wrong person in a house like this would have to be raked away, like the leaves that dropped from the trees outside. A house like this would demand a huge amount from anyone who lived in it. He didn't like it. Not at all.

He glanced at Aunt Myra and noted her tight, erect position on the edge of the little chair where she sat, her fingers hooked together as if they might never come unhooked again. Well, she'd said she'd probably be scared. But she was exclaiming on the weather, answering questions, being polite, pretending to be at her ease. Then, while Mrs. Boulderwall was pouring out the tea, the maid brought a napkin and the platter of sweets to Joe, who took a brownie. He was just wondering how soon it would be all right to eat it when Mr. Boulderwall beckoned to him. "Come on, boy," he said. "Bring that thing along to my study. We can get to know each other in there, just the two of us, while the ladies stay out here and chat."

The study was off the back of the room where they'd been sitting, and it had a door of its own which Mr. Boulderwall closed behind them when he and Joe had gone inside. A big desk and a couple of chairs took up some of the space, but mostly it was a room full of books and papers and files—on the desk, on shelves, even on the floor. It was messy, thank goodness. Not careful. Maybe Mr. Boulderwall told the housemaids to stay away. Maybe he told *Mrs.* Boulderwall to stay away. Joe took a bite of his brownie and decided to be comfortable.

Mr. Boulderwall pointed him to a chair and sat himself down behind the desk. He squinted at Joe for a moment or two and then he said, "So . . . Joe, is it? All right. You never knew your mother and father, is that the way of things?"

"Yes," he answered, aware that the irritated feeling had arrived quite suddenly, pushing aside his comfort.

"So you didn't know they were Polish," said Mr. Boulderwall.

"My grandmother never talks about things like that," said Joe.

"She's not Polish herself?"

"I don't know," said Joe. He took another bite of the brownie and added, around his mouthful, "Like I said, she never talks about it."

"Umm," said Mr. Boulderwall. "Well, I could find out her name before she got married, I suppose, but it doesn't really matter. It's just that *I'm* Polish, so you and I have something important in common. Except—I was born over there. I've been in America almost all my life, but still, the place where you're born, it's always special, even if you don't remember it." He paused, and then: "You're living with her, your grandmother. Right? You've always lived with her? So where is that? Where's home for you?"

Joe chewed up the bite of his brownie and swallowed. And then he said, "Up on Lake Erie. Willowick."

"I know where that is. East of Cleveland, right? And she's up there, waiting for you to come back?"

"Well, not exactly," said Joe. "She's in the hospital. She broke her hip on the attic stairs."

"For goodness' sake!" said Mr. Boulderwall. "That's no fun! I'm sorry to hear that. So you had to come down here alone." He got up from his chair and went to stand at a window, looking out at what had turned into a steady patter of rain. "You get along all right with her? Your grandmother?" he asked. "She's been good to you?"

"Well . . . sure!" said Joe. "Why wouldn't she be?"

Mr. Boulderwall turned around. "No particular reason," he said. Then he squinted at Joe again. "How're you doing at school?" he demanded. "You get decent grades?"

"School?" Joe exclaimed, once more surprised. "What do you want to know *that* for?" He wanted to say "It's none of your business," but managed not to.

Mr. Boulderwall tilted his head. "I want to know

because I'm interested in *you*, Joe Casimir!" he said. "Why else?"

The old man's calm, and his power, were evident. It was easy to see he was used to getting his way. But then Joe remembered Rover and the cinnamon roll. There wasn't anything to get in a fuss about with this rich old man, he told himself. He'd have to be polite, sure, but he didn't have to lean in or look hopeful, like Rover. Hopeful of what, anyway? "My grades are okay, I guess," he said. "Mostly As and Bs."

"Good," said Mr. Boulderwall. "I'm glad to hear it. And what do you want to do when you're grown up? After you're out of college? How do you want to spend your life?"

But this was farther than Joe was willing to go. He scratched at an elbow and said, looking away, "I don't know yet."

"Well, never mind," said Mr. Boulderwall. "There's plenty of time to talk about that. Because we'll be talking, Joe Casimir. We'll get to be friends. The thing is, you never had a father to share things with, and I never had a son, so we can fill in some blank spots for each other. How does that sound?"

"All right," said Joe.

"Good," said Mr. Boulderwall. He rubbed his hands together and smiled. "Well! It looks like we have that big dog to thank for all this. It's lucky he brought you here for breakfast yesterday. Dogs always make a difference, one way or another, seems to me, but I haven't had one in years. Have you got a dog? Up there in Willowick?"

"For a while I did," said Joe. "He was really my grandmother's, though. An old bulldog named Big Mike. But he had sort of a weak stomach, and used to throw up a lot, so we didn't get another one after he was gone."

Mr. Boulderwall laughed and looked at Joe with obvious satisfaction. "Probably a good decision. So! Back to the ladies. I hope they haven't eaten all the cookies."

•

It was soon over—proper thank-yous and proper goodbyes, with handshakes and bobbing of heads, and the mirror in the front hall glad to see them leaving—and then Joe and Aunt Myra were escaping through the rain. "Whew!" said Aunt Myra, turning the little black Ford into High Street. "I'm a wreck! I don't know how *your* visit went, but mine was uphill all the way. What did Mr. Boulderwall have to say?"

"He wanted to know if I get good grades in school," Joe told her, "and what I want to do when I get out of college. He says if my name is Casimir, I must be Polish. He's from Poland, too, and he said we should be friends."

"Friends?" she exclaimed. "Because you're Polish? We do have some Polish ancestors, way back, but so do a lot of people over here. I don't see what that's got to do with anything. Oh, well, when he's ready, I guess he'll let you know what's on his mind. It's kind of strange, though. Don't you think so? It seemed as if that tea party was meant just for you and him. Mrs. Boulderwall was perfectly polite, but she didn't say anything about wanting to be friends with *me*, and that's all right—I didn't expect anything—she was only passing the time. But . . . oh, Joe, what a house! What a *house*!" They had come to Glen Lane by that time, and as they were pulling into Aunt Myra's driveway, she said, "It's a whole different world up there on High Street, isn't it? That house—I can't get over it!"

"I like your house better," said Joe. He climbed out of the car, pulling off his necktie, and there in the rain, he started to stuff it into a pocket. But then he remembered the little stars all over it. He started again, folding it carefully this time, and once they were in the house, he went to his room and hung it over a hook in the closet.

VII

THE NEXT MORNING, Monday morning, Joe and Aunt Myra were just finishing an ordinary breakfast of orange juice and cereal, both of them still yawning, when there was a banging at the back door and Vinnie burst in, waving a newspaper. "Hey!" he said to Myra. "Yer a teacher, so, okay, here's somethin' t'teach! Lookit." And he pointed to an article on a folded-back inside page of the *Midville Informer*. "It's talkin' about accidents ya can't do nuthin' about, and it says how, over in England last Christmas in some town called Barwell, wherever *that* is, a big rock, and I mean a *really* big rock, fell right outta the sky and wrecked two houses! And a *car*! Oh! Hey—breakfast! Got any coffee ready?" Then, to Joe: "So, kid. How ya doin'?" He pulled out a chair from the table and flopped into it, tossing the newspaper onto the floor.

Myra fetched a mug from a cupboard, filled it with coffee, and set it down in front of him. "I'm so sorry!" she said to him. "I just plain forgot you were invited."

"Aw, c'mon, Myra," he pleaded, spooning sugar into the steaming mug. "Don't do like that! I got a great story for ya! Listen! What's in the paper reminded me of somethin' I ain't thought of in *years*! I never told ya about my granddaddy, did I? My old man's pop? Born up northeast of here, back before the Civil War. *Long* time ago. Near that town called New Concord. By the time I come along, a'course, he was gettin' pretty old, but we useta go visit him sometimes. Him and me was good friends, considerin'. He was a great old geezer. Lived his whole life on that same farm. So, listen to this! He useta tell me back then, when I was a little kid, how one day when *he* was a little kid, this humdinger of a rock, like that one they got there in the paper, come crashin' straight down outta nowhere and bopped his favorite horse! Got 'er between the ears and knocked 'er over dead. Right there in front of 'im!"

Joe sat forward, openmouthed, and Myra said, "Vinnie, for goodness' sake! That's terrible!"

"You bet! Enough to scare yer pants off, is what!" said Vinnie. He sat back in his chair and sipped his coffee thoughtfully, and then he went on: "The poor old guy! He loved that horse! Seems like he never did get over what happened to 'er, even after all those years. But the thing is, a *rock*, all by *itself*, is what finished 'er off. No announcement aheada time, no fuss and feathers, *nuthin'*. Just all of a sudden, *BAM!*—like that!" And he brought his fist down on the tabletop so hard that the cereal spoons jumped in their bowls.

Joe could keep himself quiet no longer. "It must've been a meteorite," he said. "That happens everywhere. They fall out of the sky once in a while and smash things."

"Yep," said Vinnie. "That's exactly what the paper says. What's their name again?"

"Meteorites," said Joe. "It means a meteor that's come down to earth."

"Well, okay, but what *is* it?" Vinnie demanded. "Just a big, dumb rock that busted offa somethin' up there or what?"

"It's a rock, all right, but they don't know for sure where it comes from," said Joe. "All they say is, it's not from outer space the way they used to think. It's more like—local." And then he looked away, suddenly wanting to end this conversation.

But Vinnie was nodding with approval. "This is one smart kid ya got here, Myra," he said. And to Joe he added, "Where'd ya find that out, all that? At school?"

"Oh," said Joe, looking down into his cereal bowl, "no—I guess I just read it somewhere. In a library book or something."

Vinnie swallowed the rest of his coffee and stood

up. "Stuff like that oughta get taught in school," he said. "It's important. If my granddaddy'd been the one that got bashed instead of his horse, I prob'ly wouldn't even *be* here now. I mean, ya don't see or hear them sky rocks comin' at ya. Kinda hard to get outta the way in time! Anyway, thanks for the coffee, Myra. I gotta go to work." And then he disappeared through the back door. But he left his copy of the *Midville Informer* behind on the floor.

Joe picked it up. "Okay if I keep this?" he asked Aunt Myra. "It's kind of interesting—you know—that story Vinnie told us."

"Of course you can keep it," she told him. "Meteorites. They're amazing. But it's too bad about the horse."

•

AN HOUR OR SO AFTER this conversation in Aunt Myra's kitchen down on Glen Lane, another conversation was under way in a bedroom up on High Street where the Boulderwalls were dressing for the day. "Anson, you can't be serious!" Mrs. Boulderwall was saying, her face pale, her jaws tight. "That's utterly impossible! What would Ivy say? What would all our friends say? You must be out of your mind! Adopt that common little nobody? *Adopt* him and leave him our money? And our name?"

"Calm down, Ruthetta," said Mr. Boulderwall, who was as calm as ever, himself. "I just had a birthday, remember? I'm seventy-one. I'm getting old. So are you. In a few years, it's going to be time to put somebody else in my office down at the factory. But I'm not going to turn it over to just anybody. I came awake this morning with my mind made up: I want that boy. And I want him to be with us while he's still young enough for me to train him. It'll take a while, yes. But he's plenty smart. Anyone can see that. I'll bring him along slowly, and by the time he's through college, he'll know how to do things right. Ruthetta, listen. Everything about it is so perfect! When he's ready to take over, I'll be ready to retire. More or less. Also, he's got next to no family ties to get in the way—no money-hungry relatives wanting in on the game. There's only a grandmother and this aunt or cousin or whatever she is that lives here in Midville. That seems harmless enough! And then, too, Ruthetta, he's *Polish*. I suppose I'm being sentimental, caring about that, but there's nothing wrong with a little sentiment. It feels good. It feels right. It feels like he could really be my grandson."

Mrs. Boulderwall sank down into a brocade-upholstered chair near her bed and stared at her husband. "So," she managed to say, "you're going to take Ivy's money away from her and give it to an absolute *nobody* and then just walk away."

"Ruthetta," said Mr. Boulderwall, his voice heavy with patience, "you're not listening. I'm not going to touch Ivy's money. I have another kind of plan altogether. Of course, I'll have to talk to the lawyers about it, clear the way and all, but it's my factory and I intend to pick the next president myself—pick him now, once and for all, and in writing—someone who'll follow along when the time comes and do things the way I want them done. I'm ready to pick Joe Casimir for the job, and it'll look better—he'll have more authority—if he's a legal, adopted member of my family. Joseph Casimir Boulderwall.

Sounds good to me! And when he takes my place, he'll get a good share of the stock, and a healthy salary, too—and turn into a somebody in no time at all."

Mrs. Boulderwall said, in a voice full of disgust, "A *somebody*? Somebody where? Somebody how? This boy you're so set on, and that simple-minded woman he's staying with, don't have the least idea how to fit in with people like us."

"My dear," said Mr. Boulderwall, "if I may remind you. When *we* started out, we didn't have the least idea how to fit in, either. We had to learn how to be people like us. And Joe can learn, too."

"No, he can't," she sniffed. "There isn't anyone to teach him."

"You could do it," said Mr. Boulderwall.

"Me?" she said. "*Oh* no! Not me. Not on your life. Just go on down to your office, Anson. Maybe a good day's work will bring you back to your senses."

•

THINGS MAY HAVE stayed a little cranky up on High Street, but the rest of Monday down on Glen Lane slipped away peacefully. Joe and Aunt Myra talked to Gran on the telephone in the afternoon. She had finished with the hospital, thank goodness, and was in the rehab center, working hard with exercises and doing fine, learning how to use a thing called a walker, and practicing with a couple of canes as well. Then Joe, wandering idly about, discovered a hammock put away in the garage, and when he and Aunt Myra strung it up between two trees in the backyard, it made a good place to read a book, especially if it was a book he *wanted* to read. He had found one like that on a shelf in the living room—a square-shaped book with an interesting title, *The Sky: A History*—and it was full of diagrams, charts, and photographs. In fact, there was a lot more to *look* at in this history than there was to read. But that was okay. More than okay. He lay back in the hammock, with one leg dangling over the edge so that his toe could touch the ground and keep the hammock swinging, just a little, drowsily back and forth, while he studied page after page. And then, somehow, the book slid from his fingers and dropped across his chest, and he had swung himself off into a comfortable dream in which the hammock—with him aboard—went drifting up beyond the treetops, high up, into a diagram of stars—all with five points—precisely arranged in constellations.

And then a hand was smoothing his hair, and Aunt Myra's voice was saying, "Joe! Wake up, Joe—supper's ready! Hot dogs, potato salad, all the extras! Chocolate milk, too, if you want it."

Of course he wanted it! *And* all the extras. A very fine thing to wake up to. They took their time with eating, and then, just as twilight was dropping down through the trees and they had started to discuss the serious question of dessert, the telephone rang. Aunt Myra answered it, and after a short conversation, she said to the caller, "I'll see what he thinks and get right back to you." She hung up the receiver and turned to Joe. "That was Amanda Sope—Beatrice's mother, remember?" she told him. "Rover got out of his yard again. She says he probably went across the park to where a poodle lives that he likes to visit. Gil usually hikes over there to bring him back—it isn't very far—but he and Vinnie had to go downtown to fix some kind of electrical problem at a restaurant, and Evangeline and Dorothea both have a bunch of mosquito bites and aren't very happy, so she doesn't want to leave them. But someone has to go. It's against the law for dogs to be in the park without their owners. So Beatrice will have to do it. But Mrs. Sope doesn't want her to go alone, now that it's getting dark. She says she hates to ask, but she'd feel a lot better if you went along. How about it?"

"Sure. That'd be okay," said Joe. Okay? Yes. It would be okay.

•

"It's really nice of you to do this," said Beatrice to Joe, winding Rover's empty leash around her hand as they started off down Glen Lane. "Mom always worries when one of us has to do stuff alone. But Rover goes across the park all the time, every chance he gets, and somebody always has to bring him back. It's like he's got a crush on that poodle over there, always trying to sneak out to see her the way he does."

"Does she get out, too?" Joe asked. "I mean, are they—like—friends?"

"Nope," said Beatrice. "Her yard's got a high metal fence. The people that own her—Mr. and Mrs. Macarthur—would never in the world let her out to play with a mutt like Rover. You have to have a pedigree before you're allowed to play with Tulip. That's her name. Tulip. Every time they see Rover over there, they call us up and tell us to come right away and get our *ah-nimal*, just like they were living up on High Street."

"Mr. Boulderwall called him that, too," said Joe. "Except, well, not *ah-nimal*, maybe . . ."

"No," she answered, "he wasn't stuck up about it. But Rover *is* an animal. So is Tulip. Us, too, if it comes to that. Hey, didn't you go to the Boulderwalls' yesterday? What was it like?"

"Oh—well," said Joe, "it was okay, I guess. We went inside the house, and it was pretty incredible—full of all kinds of fancy stuff—but if I lived there, I'd feel like I had to change my socks every five minutes and keep my gloves on. I'd go nuts in a house like that. I mostly talked to Mr. Boulderwall, though—

in a separate room he called his study. He asked a lot of questions."

"Like what?" she wanted to know.

He hesitated—and then found that the closed door inside his head was opening at last. He wanted to tell her. It was time. And so: "He asked me what I was going to do when I get out of college," he began. "He asked me how I want to spend my life."

"That's a pretty hard question," she said with a frown. "At least, it would be for *me.* I'd have too many different answers! So—but, what did you tell him? *Do* you know what you want?"

They had reached the farthest edge of the park. There were fewer trees here, and a green-painted bench set near the street was empty, now that the day was over. Joe sat down on the edge of it and looked up, above the rooftops and the interfering streetlights, to where a glow behind a serving of clouds gave away the secret that the moon was there, waiting for its own time onstage. Joe resisted the impulse to beckon to it. Instead, he took a deep breath and said to Beatrice, "I do know what I want.

I guess I've known ever since I was little. I want to be a scientist, and try to find a way to make sure nothing bad ever happens to change the moon. I want it to stay the same. And never ever go away."

Beatrice sat down beside him, her hands clasped under her chin. "Wow!" she said. "That sounds really good!"

"I didn't tell Mr. Boulderwall about it, though," he said, and then added, swallowing hard, "I've never told anyone before."

"Of course not!" she exclaimed. "It's nobody's business but yours. Not yet, anyway. But thank you for telling *me*." And then, "Joe," she added, "what do you think *might* happen? To the moon, I mean."

Joe leaned back on the bench, his hands in his pockets. It felt so fine to talk, at last, about all this! "Bad stuff's been going on up there since the beginning," he told her. "I've read about it a lot. The moon's really old—something like four and a half billion years old—you probably knew that already—and asteroids and comets and things've been smashing into it all that time. So it's got craters on it everywhere. But, look—I don't suppose it'll ever exactly go *away*. I mean, there's nowhere for it to go *to*! Still, it'd be good if it could be protected—if there was some way to make things go *past* it instead of into it. They're always talking about trying to do that for Earth, but we should do it for the moon, too. And I want to be in on that. Finding out how to protect it."

As he was saying this, the clouds were dissolving, and the moon, its moment come, revealed itself at last. It had begun its slow monthly waning already, but still, it seemed enormous, so low in the sky, and shapeless shadowy patches gave its face a surface that looked carelessly dabbed at here and there by a soft brush full of soft gray paint.

Beatrice said, "What makes those dark spots?"

"Some of them are mountains," he told her, "but mostly, they're sort of scooped-out places made by the stuff that crashes there. They're called impact craters. Isn't that a great name? Impact craters! So—that's what I want to do when the time comes. Ten or fifteen years from now, or thereabouts. I don't know why Mr. Boulderwall should care. But Aunt Myra said if there was anything on his mind, he'd probably let me know when he was ready."

"He likes you," said Beatrice. "Remember how I said he kept looking at you, the other day?" After a pause, she added, "I guess I should start making up my mind what *I* want to be. Oh, well, it can wait a little longer. First things first. Let's go get Rover." She stood, then, and pointed across the street. "That poodle, Tulip, lives right over there. In that big yellow house." And then, suddenly, out from behind the big yellow house, Rover, all grins and wags, was bounding across the quiet street to greet them.

"It looks like he was expecting us," said Joe.

"Maybe," said Beatrice, "but my guess is Tulip told him to mind his manners and go back where he belongs."

•

UP ON HIGH STREET, the Boulderwalls were getting ready for bed. They hadn't talked much to each other all evening, but now Mr. Boulderwall, watching his wife as she brushed her hair, said to her, "Ruthetta, I have something to tell you. At the office this afternoon, I called and made an appointment to go over to the capital tomorrow and talk to an adoption lawyer."

Mrs. Boulderwall put down her hairbrush and looked at his reflection in her dressing table mirror. "An adoption lawyer? Already?" she exclaimed. "You're really serious about all this, aren't you?"

"I really am," he told her, "and it's a huge relief. I've been worried about the factory for a long time, as you very well know, and now all at once that boy appears out of nowhere and everything falls into place. Yes. I'm convinced this is the way to go."

"All right. I guess I'm not surprised," she said. She turned around to face him. "The factory is your affair, after all, and you know best what to do with it. But *my* life is *my* affair, Anson. I've worked hard to get it right and I don't want changes. So here's how I see the situation. Use your influence and get that rinky-dink boy into a top eastern prep school starting this fall. Groton, maybe, or Exeter. Pomfret. Andover.

One of those. He'll hate it, but a good one will pull him into shape so he'll be ready for the right university and the right life afterward. He'll have to be here in the house now and then, I suppose, when you've adopted him, but the less *I* have to do with him, the better. And this way, most of the time he'll be off in New England. That should take care of things, and then, later on, when he's heading up the factory, you can find a well-bred girl for him to marry who can show him how to deal with social situations. But I'm not going to be his teacher, Anson. As long as he doesn't get in Ivy's way, he's nothing but hired help to me. A great big zero."

"As you will, my dear," said Mr. Boulderwall. "Consider it done." And he climbed happily into his bed.

"There's just one thing," she said to him as she lifted the covers of her own bed gracefully and arranged herself under them. "Have you thought about what you'll do if that boy doesn't want any part of all this?"

Mr. Boulderwall chuckled as he settled into his

pillows. "You mean, if he doesn't want the best schools in the country and then an easy job that will make him a High Street millionaire? Somehow I just don't see it turning out like that."

"I suppose you're right," she said with a sigh. "That's that, then. Have a good sleep."

And he did have a good sleep—very good indeed.

VIII

THE NEXT FEW DAYS on Glen Lane—Tuesday, Wednesday, and Thursday—were typical lazy days of the kind that sometimes make up summer vacations. Nothing to rush around for, no reason to do much but yawn and read and use up the ice cream and popcorn, and on Wednesday—this particular Wednesday for Joe, at any rate—go across the street to help Beatrice take Evangeline and Dorothea down to the park to do seesaws and swings. "If you were back home," said Beatrice to Joe with a sigh, "you'd probably be going swimming in Lake Erie, wouldn't you, or playing baseball or something, instead of helping out with all this babysitting," which of course brought on an explosive protest from Dorothea, who said flat out that, thank you very much, she was *not* a baby like *Evangeline*, which of course made Evangeline heave a handy—and muddy—clump of dandelion roots at Dorothea. Just typical lazy days.

There were telephone conversations with Gran, too, who was finally finishing her therapy—was, she insisted, hardly limping at all—and would be going home Friday for a week or two of practice with her canes and her walker before her trip down to Midville. And Joe, who was as eager now to stay in Midville as he'd been before to stay in Willowick, was telling her he was fine. She should take her time, there wasn't any hurry.

•

AND ALL THE WHILE, through these three lazy days, there was something enormous headed toward them. Something *huge*. A meteor, a comet, an asteroid—some kind of sky rock, anyway. Not a real sky rock, of course—the post office doesn't send out sky rocks—but that's what it might as well have been. Up on High Street, the Boulderwalls knew it was on its way and were waiting to see what kind of crater it would make when it hit. But down on Glen Lane, and up north in Willowick, there wasn't the slightest hint of anything. "No announcement aheada time," as Vinnie would have said. "No fuss and feathers, *nuthin'*—because ya don't see or hear them sky rocks comin' at ya." There would only be, all at once, a sudden total astonishment, an arrival out of nowhere—*BAM!*—and no sweet old horse to take the impact.

The sky rock came into sight when the telephone rang early Friday morning. It was Gran, her voice rushed, puzzled, angry: "Myra? Is that you? What in the world's going on down there?"

"Gran? What do you mean? What's wrong?"

"What's wrong? I'll tell you what's wrong! I just got a special delivery letter, and it's the biggest shock I ever had—*that's* what's wrong! I simply can't believe it! It has to be a joke, but—well, I needed to talk to you right away!"

"Slow down, Gran. What letter? What're you talking about?"

"I thought maybe *you* could tell *me,*" she declared. "This man, Anson Boulderwall—who does he think he is, for pity's sake? Oh, I know the name, of course. Who doesn't? He's always on those lists they put in the paper about the richest men in the state. But so what? Just because he's rich, that doesn't give him the right to mess with Joe like this."

"You got a letter from Mr. *Boulderwall*? About *Joe*?"

"No, the letter's from some high-and-mighty lawyer in Columbus. But it was Mr. Boulderwall that got him to write it, and it certainly is about Joe!"

"You'd better read it to me, Gran," said Myra. "Now. Every word."

"Yes," she agreed. "Good. Here goes."

FORSYTHE, WAMBAUGH & LOEB
1800 OPHAMORE AVENUE, SUITE 1228
COLUMBUS, OHIO

JUNE 17, 1965

Mrs. Roberta Casimir
1943 Lake Shore Boulevard
Willowick, Ohio

Dear Mrs. Casimir:

Our firm has been selected to represent Mr. Anson Boulderwall of Midville, Ohio, in a matter which concerns the future of your grandson, Joseph Casimir, currently residing in Midville with Miss Myra Casimir.

Mr. Boulderwall is a man of substantial means who is held in high esteem by all who know him. He is the President and owner of Swervit, Inc., as well as a loving husband and father. I relate these facts preliminary to informing you that Mr. Boulderwall, having recently made the acquaintance of your grandson, has determined, on the basis of his judgment of Joseph, to underwrite the boy's future education and training with an end to placing him, at the proper time, in a position of leadership at Swervit, Inc. This is, as I believe you will agree, an extraordinary undertaking on Mr. Boulderwall's part. I can assure you that he has the means to fulfill it completely on the boy's behalf.

In order to make this plan most effective, we have advised Mr. Boulderwall that adoption papers should be drawn up at the earliest opportunity, and he agrees. According to the public record, you are the named guardian of Joseph, having been so designated following the demise of both his parents in August of 1953. Therefore I write to request a meeting with you at your earliest convenience so that I may fully disclose the details and size of Mr. Boulderwall's generosity and can arrange for the necessary legal action to place the plan fully into effect.

I would be happy to call on you at a time of your choosing to discuss any aspect of this proposal.

Sincerely yours,
J. Converse Forsythe, Esq.

cc: Anson Boulderwall

"There! See? What do you make of *that*?" Gran exclaimed.

After a moment, Myra said softly, "I didn't know about any of this. Good grief."

"My dear," said Gran, "there's nothing good about grief, as you and I have reason to know. Look—I'm going to pull things together and come down to you tomorrow. You were expecting both of us anyway, Joe *and* me, weren't you?"

"Yes, of course I was," said Myra, "but—I mean—can you manage it? What do your doctors say?"

"My doctors?" Gran snorted. "I'm not going to discuss this with my doctors! I'm coming down to Midville tomorrow, no matter what, and that's the beginning and the end of it."

"Oh dear," said Myra. "But—Gran—how are you *feeling*? A long bus ride won't be much fun for that hip of yours, even if it is the most direct way to get here."

"No bus," said Gran. "I had plans from the beginning to come in a car. I'll just set it up for tomorrow instead of sometime in a week or two. There's a woman up here—Helen Mello, a widow like me—you met her one of those times you came visiting, I think. She's a silly old twit, but I love her dearly—we've been friends for years—and she's got a son near you, over in Oxford. She told me, when she came to see me in the hospital, that she'd drive me down to your house whenever I was ready, then go see him and his family for a couple of days and, after that, bring Joe and me back up home together. She said Oxford's practically next door to Midville."

"True enough," said Myra. "All right—come ahead. We certainly need to talk, and the sooner the better. But, Gran, shall I tell Joe what's going on? Or should I wait till you and I can tell him together?"

"Mmmm," said Gran, mulling it over. And then: "You'll have to tell him I'm coming, anyway, so I guess you'd better tell him why. I'll give you a call tomorrow afternoon from somewhere on the road when we get close. Goodbye for now. I'm going to go set things up with Helen and then start getting ready."

"All right," said Myra. "Thanks, Gran. See you soon."

•

BREAKFAST WAS READY on the table when Joe appeared, tousled and smiling. Myra found herself looking at him in a new way: Joseph Casimir *Boulderwall*? Maybe there was such a thing as good grief after all! But she put the notion firmly aside and said to him, "Hey there—you're up! Gran called a little while ago. Did the phone wake you? She's feeling a lot better, and she's coming tomorrow for her visit. She said a friend of hers—Mrs. Mello—is going to give her a ride."

Joe's smile disappeared. He sat down at his place and picked up his glass of orange juice. "Oh. Yeah. Mrs. Mello. I stayed with her when Gran went to the hospital." He looked off to one side and asked, carefully, "Will she be here for the visit, too? Mrs. Mello?"

"No, she'll be staying with her son over in Oxford," said Aunt Myra. "But she's planning to drive you and Gran back home a few days later."

"That's all right, then," said Joe, and his smile returned—but only briefly. "Hey, wait a minute! How come Gran wants to come down now?" he said. "I thought we still had a few weeks to go!"

"Well . . ." Aunt Myra reached across the table and took his hand, and her voice carried with it the faintest of trembles. "The thing is, Joe, something's happened. Something none of us could ever have expected. Joe, Gran got a letter this morning, and she's really upset. It's Mr. Boulderwall. He wants to—well, he's hired a lawyer, and he's got a plan all made to—to—oh, Joe, dear Joe, he wants to adopt you!"

BAM.

IX

WITH GRAN EXPECTED the very next day, there was a lot to do to get ready. But chores were the easy part. The hard part, for Joe and Aunt Myra, was to leave it all unspoken—not mention what was happening, not discuss Mr. Boulderwall's plan, not try to figure things out together. Because it was better to wait for Gran. Gran would know how to handle things. They agreed on that without a word. And anyway, what could they have said to each other now? What could they have said that would help? When the world you're used to, that same old world you thought you knew so well, turns itself suddenly upside down, what can you do? Everything comes tumbling off the shelves of your expectations; nothing fits anymore. So they didn't say what they wanted to say, or ask each other any of those questions, the questions that were popping in their heads like flashbulbs. Instead, they kept their eyes away from each other and concentrated on the easy part: the chores.

"You'd better sleep in the guest room, Joe." This from Aunt Myra. "It's what I said before— it'll be better for Gran if she doesn't have to climb any stairs."

Joe said, "Sure—that's all right. And don't worry about my stuff—I'll take care of it."

But he didn't ask her, "Do we have to do what Mr. Boulderwall says? What if I don't *want* to get adopted? Would I have to go live in that stuck-up house on High Street? Would I be really rich? Would that be good? Or bad?"

Aunt Myra said, "I guess we'd better strip your bed now, Joe, and I'll make one up for you in the guest room. That way, there'll be less to do in the morning. Does that sound okay? You can have either one of the guest beds." And then she added, "When that's done, I think I'll call Vinnie and see if he can find us an air conditioner for Gran, in case the nights start getting warm."

But she didn't say, "I can't let them take you away . . . I want you too much . . . I need you to finish doing your growing up right here, with me."

•

IN THE MIDDLE of the afternoon, Joe was collecting things to carry upstairs when Vinnie struggled through the door to his room, Gran's room now, hauling an enormous cardboard carton in his arms—a carton labeled *FAN-FAIR Whisper-Cool,* and below that, *Window Air Conditioner.* "Hey there, kid," said Vinnie. "Looky here! I got 'er cheap! Last year's model." He bent with a groan and lowered the carton carefully to the floor. "This'll keep yer granny perked up. Myra says the old girl busted a bone."

Joe was relieved to have something to think

about, something to talk about, that didn't involve Mr. Boulderwall. He sat down on the bed beside his half-full suitcase and said to Vinnie, "I never broke a thing. Did you?"

Vinnie knelt on the floor and began to pry open the air conditioner carton. "As a matter a'fact I did," he said, "but it wasn't that big a deal. I was just a little kid. Five or maybe six. Fell off the roof in a thunderstorm and busted my arm."

"You were on a roof in a thunderstorm?" said Joe, amazed. "You must've been really scared up there!"

"Scared? What for? Nuthin' t'be scared of. I climbed up outta my bedroom window so's I could see the lightning better. I was hangin' on to the chimney bricks when I lost my grip and slid backwards right off the edge. Landed down below in a wheelbarrow fulla rain." He grinned, remembering. "My maw really come unglued *that* time. She nailed my window shut!" He began to pull packing paper out of the carton, and soon, when the air conditioner was freed, he lifted it out and kicked the carton aside, setting the machine under one of the windows. "Now, there's one doozie of an item!" he said, staring down at its many slits and shutters and knobs, and its classic rock-gray color. "These contraptions pull alotta juice, once they get goin'. It's worth it, though, if we get one a'them hot spells."

"Sure. But, Vinnie," said Joe, "tell me more about lightning."

Vinnie eased himself down into the desk chair and rubbed his shoulders. "Not much t'tell," he said, gazing off into the distance. "It's just I always kinda thought it was *beauty*-ful. Ya know? And sudden . . . and *scary*! I really liked the scary part. I was always lookin' for someone to tell me how it worked. Had to wait for high school till I found any answers. Turned out it's just—plain old electricity! That's all it is. But them bolts can be hotter than the outside part of the *sun*, didja know that? And we didn't invent 'em or nuthin'. They're just . . . there, doin' their thing."

"And now," said Joe, "electricity's your whole business!"

"Yep," said Vinnie. "That's about the size of it. So—how about you, kid? What gets *you* goin'?"

Joe hesitated, and then said it straight out: "I want to do some kind of science about the moon. To save it from getting any more bashed up than it already is."

"Try t'keep them sky rocks from rammin' inta it," said Vinnie, nodding. "It sounds good, but ya better hurry up, kid. That moon a'yours might need more savin' than ya think, and not from no sky rocks, neither. There's alotta talk about goin' up there in rocket ships and walkin' on it, takin' pictures 'n collectin' stuff 'n figurin' it all out. Next thing, they'll find a way t'get some air up there for breathin', and then they'll start movin' *people* in. And once they do *that*, the Gobble House folks'll be right behind 'em. *Oh* yeah. Openin' up for business. I can just see it. Moonburgers! Sky Fries!" He sighed and shook his head. "We oughta leave stuff alone. New don't always mean better. Oh, well, I guess I should get this gizmo set up."

Joe stuffed a pile of socks into his suitcase, and

then he said, "Vinnie, where's the house you lived in when you fell off the roof that time? It'd be fun to go look at it. Is it on this street?"

Vinnie had opened a window and was standing in front of it, hands on hips, matching it to the air conditioner with one eye open, one eye closed. "Nowhere near," he said. "That was clear over t'Zanesville, where I grew up. Too long a drive from here, just t'go look at a roof. I didn't move t'this town till . . ." He paused, and then finished: "Till after that war we was in." He turned and, coming over to the bed where Joe was sitting, plunked down beside him. "Listen, kid, Myra says she told ya about her other Joe, that she was gonna marry," he said. "So I been thinkin' ya oughta know that him and me got t'be friends when we was in the army together, in Korea, way before I ever knew Myra. He talked t'me a lot about her. He was a great guy—one a'the best I ever knew. He got hisself killed keepin' a few of us safe with grenades when we was attacked in the dark one night. After, when I got outta the service, I come down here t'Midville t'find Myra, 'cause

I wanted t'talk to her, face to face, about him. She was workin' over to Sope Electric back then, some kinda secretary, savin' her money to go to teachers college over to Miami. She was as glad to see *me* as I was to see *her.* She fixed me up in the same job I got now, workin' with Gil. It's a good job, and I'm real happy with it. Been there more'n ten years, believe it or not. Myra and me, we don't talk much about Korea no more. We said it all to each other, long time ago. But it don't go away. It's still out there, holdin' on between us. So—we'll always stay friends."

•

THAT NIGHT, Joe carried his suitcase upstairs to the guest room. He'd chosen the bed that was nearest a window, for he wanted to be able to see the night sky while he was going to sleep. But would treetops block his view? No, it was all right: not a leaf or a branch in the way. And there was the moon, ready to be admired, faintly pinkish and showing only half of its circle of a self. But that was the way it was supposed to look, this time of the month.

It always looked the way it was supposed to look. Joe sat down, satisfied, and was leaning his arms comfortably on the windowsill when there was a tapping and Aunt Myra's voice: "Joe? It's me. How's the room working out?"

"It's fine," he said. "Come on in if you want to." And as she stepped through the doorway, he added, "I like it up here."

She crossed the room to the window beside him and looked out. "Nice moon," she said.

And he said, "Uh-huh. Just fine."

Aunt Myra sat down on the foot of the bed. The light was dimming now, inside and out, but Joe could sense that she was studying him. The uneasiness of the day, between them, was still there; they weren't any closer to relieving it. He sat back from the window, wondering whether he should switch on the floor lamp that stood between the beds. Maybe a bright light would help . . . but leaving it off might be better. Maybe, if it was really dark, Aunt Myra would go to bed. He hoped so. Otherwise, she might want to talk to him about Mr. Boulderwall, and he wouldn't be able to think of anything to say. Or at least he couldn't think of how to say anything that mattered.

But Aunt Myra seemed to want to talk about something. Not lawyers and adoption, however, or Mr. Boulderwall's money. Instead, she asked him, "Joe, were you always interested in night sky things?"

He had begun to feel his irritation once again, after many days without it, but it backed away. Night sky things—that seemed like a safe subject. "I guess I was always interested," he told her. "Near as I can remember, anyway."

"Then maybe you'll be the one to study astronomy," she said. "That would be something, wouldn't it? You instead of me! Except, it's mostly the moon you pay attention to, isn't it? You don't seem to care all that much about stars."

"Well, they're kind of little," he said, and then added quickly, "I know they're not *really* little—but that's the way they look from here."

"Yes, they don't seem very important," she said. "They're too far away. But the moon—well, everybody knows about the moon. I remember, a long time ago, if someone asked my mother to do something hard, she used to say, 'Why, I could no more do that than fly to the moon!' And now it looks like we'll all be flying to the moon one of these days, if we want to." She paused, and then she said, "Joe, why do you suppose it matters so much to you?"

"The moon? Oh—I don't know," he answered. "Gran says it's always been that way. I never especially thought about why. It's just . . . well . . . it's nice to know it's always *there*. That makes me feel good. I don't like things to keep changing."

"But, Joe!" she protested. "The *moon* changes! It changes all the time! That's what it's famous for!"

"I guess," he said. "But it doesn't go *away*."

There was a moment of silence. And then she said, "No, it doesn't go away," adding, in a lower voice, "People do, though."

Joe knew what she was talking about, but he asked her anyway: "How do you mean?"

"I just mean," she said, "people go away and there's nothing anyone can do about it. You can't depend on anyone to always be there."

"Gran says," he told her, "when it comes to

people, you can't count on anyone but yourself. But the thing is, I think you *can* always count on the moon. For it to *be* there, I mean. Sure, it changes, but the changes are always the same."

Aunt Myra stood up, then, and looked once more out the window at the moon. "Will you want to go up there in a rocket ship someday, do you think?" she asked him.

Joe laughed. "Nope," he said. "Not ever." And he told her what Vinnie had said about Moonburgers.

Aunt Myra laughed, herself. And then she told him, "Joe, I didn't come in here meaning to be gloomy. I'm just worried right now. I hate not knowing what to do about this business with Mr. Boulderwall—it's got me totally confused."

"Gran will know what to do," said Joe.

"Yes, that's right. Gran will have the answers," she said. "Get some sleep now, Joe, if you can. It's going to be a big few days coming up."

And then she was gone. Joe climbed out of his clothes and found a nightshirt, and was soon back sitting on the edge of his bed. Yawning, he looked out at the moon. Even with half its face in shadow, he liked to imagine that it knew they were there for each other—that he could ask it for advice and it would always know what was right. He could ask it to tell him if being rich would be a good thing—or bad. If he was very rich, could they still be friends? Then, drowsily, he stretched out under the sheets, already half asleep, and in his rising dreams he seemed to hear, from very far away, the answer to his questions: "You can have the moon or money. Money or the moon. There's no such thing as both."

X

THE TELEPHONE RANG around one thirty on Saturday afternoon. Gran. "I'm in a phone booth in Springfield," she announced to Myra. "Helen put together a picnic for our lunch and we've been eating in the car. But we're ready to get back on the highway now. Whew! Four hours is a lot of driving! But one more hour ought to do it—it's about fifty miles from here down to Midville, near as I can tell from the map."

"Oh, Gran! I'm so relieved to hear from you!"

said Myra. "How's your hip? How're you holding up?"

"Me? I'm doing all right," she responded. "Better now that I'm not just sitting around the house all upset and mad as . . . well, never mind what I'm mad as. Helen's doing all right, too, bless her! We got stopped for speeding when we were making that curve around Columbus, but she sweet-talked the officer. Apologized, and called him 'dear,' and told him how handsome he looked in his uniform. I don't think I ever saw a policeman try so hard not to smile! He let us off without a ticket. How about that! All we got was a warning. So . . . how's Joe?"

"He's fine," Myra told her. "I'd put him on, but he got restless and went out back to clean up the yard. And, Gran, we haven't talked about that letter you got. I told him what Mr. Boulderwall wants to do, but we haven't actually talked about it."

"Well," said Gran, "that's all right. Probably just as well. What I'm thinking is, we'll talk it through when I get there, up one side and down the other, see what we all think, and then I'll make an appointment with that Boulderwall man for tomorrow. I'd better get off this phone now—there's a crabby-looking girl waiting for it. So—all right! See you in an hour!"

•

BY THREE THIRTY they were together in the Glen Lane living room—Myra, Joe, and Gran, with Gran unpacked and settled in the downstairs bedroom. Mrs. Mello had helped her out of the car and walked close beside her into the house, just in case, for Gran was stumping along by means of the walker—a strange-looking, three-sided metal cage sort of thing, waist high, of no weight at all but very strong, that she could lean on and clank about in. "Why, there you are, you dear, plucky lad!" Mrs. Mello chirped when she saw Joe. And to Myra, "You must be that sweet girl Berta is so fond of! My, my! What have we here? Three Casimirs in one room! I wish I could stay and chat, but I have to get on over to Oxford to my own treasures. So I'll turn your honey of a grandma over to you both and see you later on, when it's time for us all to go home. Toodle-oo!" And off she went.

Now, with peace restored and the walker tucked into a corner, Gran was happy to claim a normal armchair at last. She sank down into it carefully, with a sigh. "Joe," she said to him, "I've missed you like crazy, but it's clear everything's been okay down here with Myra."

"Yep," said Joe. "It's been good." And then he added, "I was kind of worried, but you look just like always, Gran. I'm really glad you're okay."

"Thanks," she said, "but I'll be more okay when we figure out this adoption business. I was really in a rage yesterday when I read that lawyer's letter, but now, well, I realize it isn't just a casual suggestion, it's a flat-out offer of a completely new life for you—a kind of life I don't know anything about. I mean, it's so huge, I can't see all the way around it! So what I need to know is, what's on the other side? Once you get past the money, if you *can* get past the money, what are these people really like, these Boulderwalls? Joe, you talked to Mr. Boulderwall when you went to his house for tea, right? Tell me what you thought of him."

Joe frowned, thinking back to Mr. Boulderwall's face, the squinting eyes examining him, the short, determined questions, and at last he said, "Well, gee, I don't know, Gran. He's old, but . . . it'd be easy to be scared of him. I guess he knows what he wants, all right. But he wasn't *mean* or anything. He just had a bunch of questions about school, stuff like that, and he said we should be friends because he doesn't have a son and I don't have a father."

"Nothing about adoption?" she asked him.

"Nope," said Joe. "Not a word."

"I can't understand it," said Gran, shaking her head. "But, Myra, you talked to Mrs. Boulderwall. What about *her*? What about the way they *live*?"

"Their house is really beautiful," said Myra. "Very big, everything perfect. I liked it. But Joe didn't. He said it looked like a house in a movie. It had everything but the cameras. And in a way he was right! Mrs. Boulderwall reminded me of an *actress* in a movie. She didn't seem real. Her clothes were too elegant, and the things she said were like lines she had to learn for the part she was playing. She'd make a remark and then she'd look at me to see if I knew *my* lines and could answer back. I felt like a real clunk. That was just me, though. It's not as if she was exactly rude or anything. Still, it's funny . . . I kept thinking she was trying so hard, she didn't have time to be friendly."

"Maybe it's hard work to be rich," said Gran. "Or maybe they're just not used to ordinary people like us. Do they have any children of their own?"

"They have a married daughter up in Cleveland, but no grandchildren," said Myra.

"There's no one to take over the business, then," said Gran. "That could explain a lot. Except—why choose Joe? Why not somebody with experience, somebody the right age now? And what about *our* family? There's just the three of us, sure, but family is family . . . and, Joe, do you know anything about those little machines Mr. Boulderwall makes?"

"Swervits," said Joe. "Remember? You got a new one for your car last year."

"Well, but, Joe," she pressed him, "would you *like* a job like that? Being the boss in a factory?"

Joe looked at her troubled face, and looked away quickly. He wanted to tell her what he wanted to do—oh, how he wanted to tell her!—but he was lost in uncertainty. She was the one who was supposed to know what was best, but maybe she *didn't* know! So how should he answer her question? Would she like it if he was rich? If she didn't have to worry about money for his college? And what right did he have, anyway, to push for his own ideas when he believed, as he always had, that he should try to please her? He felt, all at once, impossibly young and helpless, and the irritated feeling filled his head. He mumbled, "I don't know what to say. I just—don't know."

•

AND THEN, BLESSEDLY, the kitchen door burst open and Vinnie's voice was calling: "Hey! Myra? Where are ya? Anybody home?"

"Oh, good," said Myra. "It's Vinnie!" And she called back, "We're here, in the living room! Come and meet Joe's grandmother!"

Vinnie came into the living room and nodded to Gran in his usual warm and easy way. "How do, ma'am," he said with a smile. "I just stopped by t'see if the air conditioner was doin' okay, and here ya sit, lookin' all settled in!" He turned to Joe, then, and said, "Hey, kid! Now ya got two to look after! Not a bad way t'spend yer time!"

But Myra interrupted this thought. "Gran!" she said. "Vinnie is one of my dearest friends, and he's gotten to know Joe, too—they've had a lot of conversations—so what would you think about bringing him into our discussion? He'll need to know what's going on sooner or later, and he's sure to have some good ideas."

"All right," said Gran. "That would be fine with me!"

"Hold on, now," said Vinnie. "What ya talkin' about? *What's* goin' on?"

Gran lifted her pocketbook from the floor beside her, unzipped it, and took out an envelope. "It's all in this letter that came to me yesterday, Vinnie, up home in Willowick. We're just trying to figure out what we ought to do."

Vinnie took the envelope and looked at the return address. "Uh-oh," he said. "Lawyers." He perched on an arm of the sofa, frowning, and slid the letter out of its envelope. And then he began to read, slowly and carefully, his expression growing more and more astonished. Coming to the end of it at last, he lifted his eyes to Joe's face. "Ya know all about this, kid?" he asked.

Joe nodded. "Pretty much," he said.

"Well," said Vinnie, "there ain't no puzzle to it. Not t'*my* mind, anyway. I mean, the old guy wants t'retire without retirin'. He's a good businessman, and he's got it all figured out. Take on the kid here, train 'im up in a few fancy schools, and then, when the time comes, stick 'im inta the office and sit back. Everyone'll expect him t'retire. I mean, it's the classy thing t'do. But it'll only *look* like he's retirin'. He'll still be the head man. He'll still tell ya what t'do. He likes ya, kid, but don't get the notion he *loves* ya. He's not doin' all this adoption stuff for love."

Vinnie handed the letter back to Gran. "Lookit," he said. "There's nuthin' wrong with money, all by itself. It just lies around stacked up in the bank. It can't make ya smart if yer dumb, and it can't keep ya straight if ya feel like cheatin'. Sure, everyone's gotta *have* some. But, kid, if ya wanna get *rich*, this could be one way t'do it. Ain't no real harm in it, far as I can see." He stood up and grinned around at them all. "How's that for advice from a guy who never had two cents t'rub together? See ya later!" And he went back through the kitchen and out the door.

They sat, then, in silence, each with different thoughts, Gran sipping her tea, Myra rubbing her chin, and Joe staring at the floor. Vinnie had driven off in the Sope Electric van and everything was quiet until, from across the street, there was barking, full-throated barking, barking to warn the world of terrible dangers and intrusions. The three in the living room looked up. "It's Rover Sope," said Myra. "He's probably seen that cat that lives around the corner. She comes over here every once in a while to check things out—don't ask me what things. She's a cat, after all. And if he sees her, he finds a way to get out of his yard and come after her. She just climbs a tree or something, though, and doesn't pay a bit of attention to him. There! He's gotten loose!"

Rover had managed to come into Myra's front yard, still barking, and on top of that, they heard someone yell to him to come home where he belonged. Beatrice! Joe got to his feet. "I'll go help get him penned up," he said. "Be right back."

•

THE CAT WAS NOWHERE to be seen when Joe went out, but Beatrice was there, fastening Rover's leash to his collar, and together she and Joe crossed the sun-splattered street, the dog between them. "I'm going to put him in the house," said Beatrice. "If I don't, he'll just get out again. Thanks for helping, Joe."

But Joe said, "Beatrice, wait—come out for a few minutes after, okay? I have to talk to you. I guess I'm not supposed to tell anyone about this, but there's something I really need to ask you. I need to know what you think."

"Well . . . sure!" she said. And in a moment, with Rover stowed inside, they sat down side by side on the grass. "So what's going on?" she asked him. And Joe took a deep breath, swallowed hard, and told her about the letter from the lawyer.

When he had finished, Beatrice pulled up a weed or two, slowly, and at last, keeping her eyes down, she asked him, "Don't you want to be a scientist anymore?"

"*Sure* I do!" he said.

Beatrice turned to look at him directly. "Well, then," she said, "where's the problem? All you have to do is say so."

Joe stared at her. "But I just . . . I mean . . . if Gran wants . . . it seemed like I had to at least think it over!"

"So you thought it over!" she said. "But you didn't change your mind. Right?"

Joe said, amazed, "You make it sound so simple!"

Beatrice smiled at him. "It *is* simple," she told him. "In spite of what anyone else has to say, it's *your* life you're talking about, Joe Casimir. Nobody else's. And you have to do what you really want to do with it."

Joe stared at her, at her smile and the way she

was looking at him, and the irritated feeling moved out from that corner of his head where it had lived for so long—moved out, stood apart, dissolved, and disappeared. He smiled back at her then and said, "Wow."

•

BACK IN AUNT MYRA'S living room, he said to the two who were waiting, "I've made up my mind. I don't want anything to do with adoption. Money can be nice, sure, but it's just not nice enough. I want to do what I've wanted to do for so long, I hardly even know when it started." And he told them all about the moon.

•

LATER, WHEN MYRA was putting together a simple Saturday night supper for the three of them, Gran clanked out to the kitchen and demanded, "Who says nobody has any sense till they turn twenty-one?"

"Not me!" said Myra. "I always have plenty of

sensible kids in my fifth-grade classes. In fact, sometimes it seems to me that the older we get, the *less* sensible we are!"

Gran nodded. "Very true," she agreed. "Take me, for instance. Right now I feel like dancing a jig!"

"So do I," said Myra with a smile. "And soon you'll be able to."

"I guess so," Gran replied with a smile of her own. "But it feels pretty fine just to *want* to!"

XI

Sunday afternoon can be a lovely time, especially in June. It isn't that Sunday is the beginning of a new week—no, Sunday is quite separate, a day off by itself, not the beginning or the end of anything. It's a time for the world, and the other six days of the week, to keep out of the way . . . unless you happen to be someone who's about to face a millionaire in his big and beautiful house on the best street in town.

Some of us, however, are fearless. Gran had

called Mr. Boulderwall on the telephone on Saturday, after Joe had said what he had to say, and in a voice she rarely used—a voice Joe was very glad she wasn't using on *him*—demanded an interview for three o'clock the next day, Sunday afternoon. And was given it. "Well, why shouldn't he agree to see me?" she said when she'd hung up the phone. "I probably sounded like his mother!" She smiled, then, a smile of enormous satisfaction, for she was deeply glad—and proud—of Joe's decision. So was Myra. And they'd said as much to Joe. To celebrate, they'd gone out to the Gobble House after supper, and all three ordered—and ate to the last spoonful—a chocolate Flipsie for dessert: a sundae with all the sauce on the bottom so that—poor you!—you had to dig for it. And later, when they went to bed on Glen Lane, all three slept the sleep that will come when the world, which had turned itself upside down, rights itself at last and becomes again the same old world you thought you knew.

Being fearless, Gran was completely calm on Sunday. When Myra asked her what she was going to wear for the interview, she only laughed. "Wear? Why, I'm going to wear the same thing I'd wear for anyone! Just a plain old skirt and blouse. With a jacket. And two canes. I'm going to use two canes instead of my walker—I learned how in rehab. They kind of thump as you go along, but that's better than clanking. And they take up a lot less room. Joe, fetch me those canes from my room, would you, please? I guess I ought to try them again before I go."

And then, after a successful practice, and closer to the deadline, the doorbell rang and there was Mrs. Mello. "Hello, all!" she chirped. "It's only me. But I have something to discuss with Berta, and I thought we could just go out for a ride and have a little chat."

"Can't do it now, Helen," said Gran. "I'm already having a little chat. With Mr. Boulderwall, that man I told you about yesterday. And I'm due up there in just a few minutes."

"No problem in the least," said Mrs. Mello. "It's High Street, right? I know where that is. I'll drive you, and then I'll just wait in the car till you're ready to leave."

"Oh, Mrs. Mello, I don't think . . ." said Aunt Myra. "I mean, I was going to do that. Maybe even go in with Gran, to act as a kind of backup."

But Gran said, "You know, Myra, this might actually be better. If Helen drives me up, you'll be completely out of it. They couldn't blame you for a thing. Whereas I can go up there, say my piece, make my noise, and leave. I don't have to worry that I'll see them somewhere after, because I won't *be* here. Yes. I like it better. Helen and I can have our own little talk in the car. And counting everything from start to finish, we'll probably be back in an hour or so for a cup of tea and some cookies. All right?"

"Well," said Myra, "I guess so. Maybe you're right. Joe, what do you think?"

But Joe had escaped outside to the backyard and was swaying in the hammock, buried once more—wide awake this time—in *The Sky: A History*.

•

THE FRONT HALL at the Boulderwalls' house looked just the same as it had a week before—more white roses, more disapproval from the heavy gilt-framed mirror. But Gran was not taken to the living room. Instead, a maid led her to a much smaller room—a sort of parlor—with roses, in smaller vases, that were pink—and here she was directed to a settee with dark-red velvet upholstery, and was left alone for a minute or two to examine her surroundings: an elaborate landscape painting framed on the wall above a marble fireplace, two chairs with their own dark red upholstery, books on a wide bookcase, windows looking out to the terrace beyond. Little tables stood handy, waiting for cups of tea—or, possibly, glasses of wine. It was a beautiful room, and yet Joe and Myra were right about this house. It looked as if it had never been lived in.

But it was *owned*, no question of *that*. Gran heard a deep voice giving orders to someone in the hall beyond the door, and then the man of the house—the rich old man of the house—stood before her. "Mrs. Casimir?" he said. "How do you do." And he looked at her closely, squinting, measuring her, but otherwise his face was without expression.

Gran looked back at him, equally expressionless.

"How do you do," she replied. "Yes, I am Roberta Casimir, Joe Casimir's grandmother and legal guardian. And you, I presume, are Anson Boulderwall?"

"I am," he replied, sitting down in one of the chairs opposite her. "I see you're using canes today. Joe told me you'd had a fall at home. It's good to find you making such a speedy recovery."

"Thank you," she answered. "Yes, I'm doing very well. And since that is the case, it seemed reasonable for me to come down to Midville and talk to you immediately, and personally, about your wish to adopt my grandson."

"You've received the letter from Columbus, then?" he asked.

"I have," she told him. "Early Friday morning, at my home in Willowick."

"Very good," said Mr. Boulderwall with a nod. "Mr. Forsythe, my lawyer, was quick to see what a fine opportunity this is for Joe. It will be so satisfying when it's put into action!"

Gran said, calmly, "A fine opportunity indeed—for *someone*. But not for Joe."

Mr. Boulderwall stared. His satisfaction vanished,

leaving him with only a slightly open mouth. "I beg your pardon," he said, leaning forward. "Perhaps I misunderstood you."

"I said," Gran repeated, "that it would *not* be a fine opportunity for Joe. He doesn't want an office job. He has other plans."

Mr. Boulderwall sat back again. "Oh, well, as to *that,* I'm sure you're mistaken. I asked him, a few days ago, what he wanted to do when he got out of college, and he told me he didn't know."

Gran smiled. "Forgive me," she said, "but he knows, all right—he just hasn't talked much about it. Not to me, anyway. Not until yesterday afternoon. And he certainly wouldn't have talked about it to a stranger."

"Oh, well, boys!" said Mr. Boulderwall. "They have their little ways. I used to be one, myself, so I ought to know!"

"What you ought to know," said Gran, "is that young people are not all alike just because they're young, boys *or* girls. I've watched over Joe ever since he was two months old—ever since his parents died.

I know him very well. Back when he was first without his mother and father—his father was my only child—Joe was lucky enough not to know what he'd lost. How could he know? He was so new to the world and so busy getting used to things!" She looked away from Mr. Boulderwall's frowning face, out through a window to the flagstones and grass of the terrace. "He was cheerful, and curious . . . and eager," she said. "But, like lots of other babies, he did cry once in a while for what seemed like no reason at all that we could see, his grandfather and I. It's possible he just wanted to be comforted. I guess everyone wants that sometimes, reason or no reason. At any rate, we kept his crib in our bedroom, near a window, so we'd be handy if he needed us at night." Then her voice, that had turned soft with memories, was firm again: "But—and this is the important thing—when the moon was shining outside that window, when it was a full moon or even only half-full, he simply didn't cry! Not once. I'd get up to see why he was so quiet, and he'd be wide awake, lying there looking out the window at the moon, and he'd be reaching his arms up to it, and smiling at it, as if it made him feel safe and happy to see it there. I'd seen him look just that way at his mother and father, arms reaching up and all, and I confess I thought briefly, back then, that maybe he saw the moon as a kind of substitute for them after they were gone. But . . . well, that's extremely unlikely, I know. I don't go in much for psychological mumbo jumbo. The world has always seemed pretty practical to me. So all I can say is that he had a real love for the night sky back then, and he still does. He says now that he wants to be some kind of scientist when he grows up—the kind that studies things in the sky, especially the moon. He wants to be in on the research that's trying to find a way to keep things like meteors and comets from smashing into us here—and also into the moon."

Mr. Boulderwall examined the knuckles of one hand for a moment, and then he looked again at Gran, his reaction to her story empty of emotion. He had become, instead, a practical man of business. "The kind of education required for scientific study is expensive," he said. "Regular undergraduate tuition at first, of course, and then four years of graduate school at the very least, with another big batch of tuition and a great many extra expenses. Have you considered all that?"

"Of course," said Gran. "His grandfather and I began putting money away for his college as soon as he was born. It may not be enough when the time comes, but he's been such a good student, he'll probably be able to get a decent scholarship right here at State."

"Correct me if I'm wrong," said Mr. Boulderwall, "but you're a widow now. Or so I've been told. There's no one but you to provide all this."

"That's so," she replied, "but it doesn't especially worry me. I'll find a way to manage when the time comes."

Mr. Boulderwall stood up abruptly and thrust his hands into his pockets. "My dear Mrs. Casimir," he said, "perhaps you don't understand what your letter from my lawyer is trying to tell you. When I adopt your grandson, money for him—for his education and everything else he will ever want or need—will never be a problem again. *Never again*. For starters, my wife and I have decided that we'll send him, this coming fall, to a first-class eastern prep school. And after that to one of the finest universities in the country. Harvard, probably. Or Yale. I doubt you'd be able to afford all that."

"You'd send him to a university," said Gran, "but not to study the sciences."

"Why—no! Of course not!" he exclaimed with growing impatience. "He'll get his regular undergraduate degree in something useful, like economics or international relations, and then he'll go on to business school and train to take over my factory! As for this moon thing, there's no real challenge there. It's only some quirk left over from his infancy. My guess is, he'll outgrow it. But if he doesn't, well, he can build his own observatory right here, in back of the house, and when he's not down at the factory, he can fool around with telescopes as much as he wants to."

"In back of the house?" Gran repeated. "Does

that mean you would expect him to live up here with you?"

"Why, certainly! At first, anyway—until he gets married. He'll be sure to want his own house when *that* time comes." Mr. Boulderwall began to walk back and forth, a baffled—and angry—frown deepening on his face. "Don't you hear what I'm saying?" he burst out at last. "I'm talking about the best of everything for that boy! For the rest of his life, he'll have all the money anyone could want! Why, to be rich—it's the American dream! Everybody loves money! It's what everybody wants! Surely you must be aware of that! To be able to live in a place like High Street—why, it's *ideal*! It's *perfection*! Everyone that sees it wants it—or a place just like it. Why can't you understand? It doesn't come true for a lot of people, of course, a dream like that—but I can make it come true for your grandson with a simple snap of my fingers! He can manage my factory exactly the way I would myself—and in exchange, I can give him a perfect life! How you can turn your back on an offer like that is simply more than I can grasp!"

"You have it the right way round at last," said Gran. She struggled to her feet, clutching her canes, and her telephone voice took over: "It does seem to be more than you can grasp. So I'll put it as simply as I can. My grandson is not for sale. Not now, not ever. He doesn't want to sit in an office every day for the rest of his life and run a business, never mind how good that business is or how much money you'd give him to do it. There are a lot of different dreams in America, Mr. Boulderwall, not just one. And Joe's dream is to learn things. Discover things. High Street could never be for him what it seems to be for you. His head is too full of questions, and they're not the kind of questions High Street can answer. He'll have to study hard for answers. He *wants* to study hard. There's a lot to be learned. Because, Mr. Boulderwall, he wants to reach up to the moon—yes—and he'll do it, too. But not to make money because of it, not to hold it in his *hands.* All he wants is to understand it—and protect it. No, my grandson is not for sale. And neither, by the way, is the moon. Goodbye."

Leaving Mr. Boulderwall in stunned silence behind her, Gran stumped out, leaning heavily on her canes, and nearly collided with a woman hovering near the parlor door. "My dear Mrs. Casimir," the woman murmured, tipping her head back and gazing at Gran through lidded eyes, "how *do* you do! I am Ruthetta Boulderwall. Mrs. Anson Boulderwall. My husband didn't want me with him while you and he were having your little wrangle, but I listened out here, and I agree with you one hundred percent. That grandson of yours doesn't belong on High Street. I never thought it was a good idea, Anson's wanting to adopt him. He's just not our kind of people."

"I'm delighted to know you think so," said Gran. "Good day."

•

"So, sweetie! Did you tell the old buzzard what's what?" asked Mrs. Mello when Gran was settled back into the car.

"Yes, I think he got my point," said Gran, "and

since I'm Joe's legal guardian, that should be the end of that!"

"Thank goodness," said Mrs. Mello. "Oh, by the way, did you meet his wife?"

"Actually, I did. Just now. She was eavesdropping on our conversation."

"Well, guess what!" said Mrs. Mello. "I got out of the car and wandered around for a few minutes to stretch my legs, and I found this under a bush where the mailman must have dropped it." And she held out a shiny folder, bright with pictures of shoes and pocketbooks. "It's only an advertisement, nothing important, but take a look at who it's addressed to, there on the back," she said to Gran.

Gran turned the folder over and read it aloud: "Mrs. Ruthetta Grumpacker Boulderwall. Okay. That must be her full name, but so what?"

"I'll tell you so what," said Mrs. Mello. "I mean, how many girls have you known with a name like Ruthetta Grumpacker?"

"I guess she's the only one," said Gran. "Not that I can say I exactly *know* her. Why?"

"Well, *I* know her," said Mrs. Mello. "Or at least I used to! We were in school together up in Clarksfield, a long ways back. We were in the fifth grade, I think it was, when her grandfather got put in jail for stealing a cow!"

"Oh, come on, Helen!" said Gran. "Why would you remember a thing like that?"

"Easy," said Mrs. Mello with a wide, delighted grin. "It was *my* grandfather's cow he stole!"

And they laughed all the way back to Glen Lane.

•

IN AUNT MYRA'S living room again, Gran happily reported on her visit with Mr. Boulderwall, and they were settling down to tea and cookies when Mrs. Mello said suddenly, "Berta! I nearly forgot what I came here to tell you! It's my son! He told me last night, they want me to come down from Willowick and move in with them—him and Jeanie, his wife! He doesn't like me living alone up on the lake, and he says their house feels empty anyway, now that their two kids are grown and gone. We've talked about something like that before, you and I—remember? But we never really expected it to happen! I hardly know what to think!"

Myra put her teacup down with a clink and leapt to her feet. "Wait!" she cried. "Don't answer that till I get a turn! Gran, that's exactly what I've been wanting to say to *you*! I want you and Joe here with me so badly, I can hardly bear it! And if Mrs. Mello is going to be that close by, maybe it wouldn't be so selfish of me after all! She'd be practically next door! Oh, Gran, there's plenty of room here, and to have your company—and take care of each other—with Joe here for both of us to love a good while longer—it would be a dream come true!"

"Hmm!" said Gran. "Our branch of the Casimir family together at last! Of course, it's possible that the Boulderwalls would make things hot for me if I was here all the time."

"But maybe not," said Mrs. Mello with a grin. "Remember, Berta, you've got a weapon of your own now. I make you a gift of it."

"What weapon?" asked Aunt Myra.

"Oh," said Gran, "just a cow that got stolen. Helen will tell you all about it one of these days. So . . . sell the Willowick house and—for goodness' sake! Of *course*! Keep most of the money for Joe to go to college! And use the rest of it to pay our share of the monthlies with our very dear Aunt Myra! Casimirs all, right here in Midville! Joe, what do you say?"

And Joe, choosing from a small but growing collection of memories of the girl across the street, thought about her smile from the afternoon before, and how she had given him back to himself, and he said, "I think it would be really, really good!"

And so it was.

EPILOGUE

THIS HAS been Joe Casimir's story, yes, but stories don't just stop. Things went on happening in Midville while Joe was upstate with Gran, getting ready to move back down at the end of the summer, and maybe some of those things didn't matter much—not to Joe, anyway—but there were three that were important enough, each in its own way, to appear on the front page of the *Midville Informer.* Beatrice Sope knew they would matter to Joe, so she clipped them out of the paper and held them for him.

The first one came out in early July:

HEROIC MUTT SAVES PEDIGREED POODLE FROM DOGNAPPER

Last evening, Mr. and Mrs. Horace Macarthur, of Kenwood Drive, came home from an early party to hear the sound of frightful snarling, barking, and yelling coming from the rear of their house. They hurried to find the cause and discovered that a stranger had cut a large hole in the wire fence of the outdoor yard of Tulip, their prizewinning poodle, and was attempting to climb through it to snatch her, while at the same time a large male mixed-breed dog had grabbed hold of his ankle with strong jaws and was trying to drag him back. Mr. Macarthur summoned the police, who arrived in minutes, and peace was quickly restored. Mrs. Macarthur was able to identify the mixed-breed male, who, she said, is a frequent visitor at the poodle's outdoor yard. He is Rover, pet of the Sope family, whose home is on Glen Lane. Mr. Macarthur told this reporter that he and his wife have often tried to shoo the dog away, but from now on he will always be given a hero's welcome.

Then, in the first week of August, this surprising announcement appeared:

FLEDGE VALVE TO REPLACE SWERVIT

It has been a full year since a pair of brothers, working in a garage near Detroit, Michigan, invented and perfected an engine attachment they call a fledge valve. And now, after extensive testing, auto manufacturers are satisfied that it will not only save the industry time and money, it will, by its new approach to the work done before by the time-honored swervit, greatly improve the safety of long-distance driving for car owners, as well as operators of buses and all types of trucks. So it appears that the swervit, invented and manufactured by Midville's own Anson Boulderwall, will soon become obsolete. The swervit factory, here in Midville, has been for forty years the only spot for manufacture of the device. However, a spokesman assures us that the space will not go to waste: The building and its various additions will be sold to Cuddlebug and Co., maker of children's toys, and it is expected that many former Swervit employees will find new work in the old location.

Mr. Boulderwall has stated that he will be selling his High Street home, and that he and Mrs. Boulderwall will move upstate to a suburb of Cleveland, where they will be near their daughter. *See story on page 15.*

And finally, there was the following brief announcement in the Labor Day edition of the *Informer*:

LOCAL MAN WINS SWEEPSTAKES

Yesterday, at the annual drawing of the statewide Buckeye Bucks Sweepstakes, Midville resident Vincent Fortunado won the first prize of one million dollars. He has told the *Informer* that he plans to use most of his winnings to purchase a home in Florida for his elderly parents, who have lived for many years in Zanesville, and he hopes, after that, to buy half ownership in Sope Electric, his employer for more than a decade.

Mr. Fortunado, known to friends as "Vinnie," told us, "It's a swell deal. I'm real happy."

So things go right on happening—some good, some bad, of course, but in this case, the good things lead the list. At least, they're good for *most* of the featured people. Probably the dognapper is saying what happened to him was bad—even if it *was* his own fault he ended up in jail with a great big bandage on his ankle. And probably Mr. Boulderwall is sorry that his factory bit the dust, even if he *is* still one of the richest men in the state. But there are no two ways about Vinnie. He has come right out and said, himself, that he's "real happy."

There's an endless future waiting. It doesn't belong to just a few of us; it belongs to everyone. And much of it can be happy if you're patient and wait your turn. It does go on forever, after all. It changes all the time, yes, but it doesn't go away; it's always there, even when you're not looking. Just like the love of money. Just like the moon.

DISCARDED BY
FREEPORT
MEMORIAL LIBRARY